about these talented authors...

Vicki Lewis Thompson

"One of the hottest Western romances of the year!"
—*RT Book Reviews* on *Claimed!*

"A visit to the Last Chance Ranch
is a great way to spend an afternoon!"
—*Fresh Fiction* on *Cowboy Up*

Jennifer LaBrecque

"Nobody writes a hot novel better
than Jennifer LaBrecque."
—*CataRomance Reviews* on *Nobody Does It Better*

"LaBrecque is an author
I highly recommend to any romance reader."
—Tonya Callihan, *Fresh Fiction*

Rhonda Nelson

"Well plotted and wickedly sexy,
this one's got it all—including a
completely scrumptious hero. A keeper."
—*RT Book Reviews* on *The Ranger*

"This highly romantic tale is filled with emotion and
wonderful characters. It's a heart-melting romance."
—*RT Book Reviews* on *Letters from Home*

New York Times bestselling author **Vicki Lewis Thompson**'s love affair with cowboys started with the Lone Ranger, continued through Maverick and took a turn south of the border with Zorro. She views cowboys as the Western version of knights in shining armor—rugged men who value honor, honesty and hard work. Fortunately for her, she lives in the Arizona desert, where broad-shouldered, lean-hipped cowboys abound. Blessed with such an abundance of inspiration, she only hopes that she can do them justice. Visit her website at www.vickilewisthompson.com.

After a varied career path that included barbecue-joint waitress, corporate numbers-cruncher and bug-business maven, **Jennifer LaBrecque** has found her true calling writing contemporary romance. Named 2001 Notable New Author of the Year and 2002 winner of the prestigious Maggie Award for Excellence, she is also a two-time RITA® Award finalist. Jennifer lives in suburban Atlanta with a Chihuahua who runs the whole show.

A Waldenbooks bestselling author, two-time RITA® Award nominee, *RT Book Reviews* Reviewers' Choice nominee and National Readers' Choice Award winner, **Rhonda Nelson** has more than twenty-five published books to her credit and thoroughly enjoys dreaming up her characters and manipulating the worlds they live in. She and her family make their chaotic but happy home in a small town in northern Alabama. She loves to hear from her readers, so be sure to check her out at www.readRhondaNelson.com.

Vicki Lewis
Thompson

Jennifer LaBrecque
Rhonda Nelson

Merry Christmas, Baby

TORONTO NEW YORK LONDON
AMSTERDAM PARIS SYDNEY HAMBURG
STOCKHOLM ATHENS TOKYO MILAN MADRID
PRAGUE WARSAW BUDAPEST AUCKLAND

ISBN-13: 978-0-373-79655-7

MERRY CHRISTMAS, BABY
Copyright © 2011 by Harlequin Books S.A.

The publisher acknowledges the
copyright holders of the individual works
as follows:

IT'S CHRISTMAS, COWBOY!
Copyright © 2011 by Vicki Lewis Thompson

NORTHERN FANTASY
Copyright © 2011 by Jennifer LaBrecque

HE'LL BE HOME FOR CHRISTMAS
Copyright © 2011 by Rhonda Nelson

Recycling programs
for this product may
not exist in your area.

CONTENTS

IT'S CHRISTMAS, COWBOY!

Vicki Lewis Thompson
A Sons of Chance *Holiday Novella*

For Jen and Rhonda—I'm honored to be in an anthology with both of you. Merry Christmas! (Does this count as a card?)

1

A RUNAWAY HORSE AND AN approaching blizzard made for a bad combo, especially the afternoon before Christmas. Tucker Rankin's eyes watered as he gunned the snowmobile in an effort to catch Houdini, a black-and-white stallion with a taste for freedom. The roar of the snowmobile and the white rooster tail it created shattered the peace and quiet of a Wyoming landscape blanketed by last week's storm.

About two hours of daylight remained, and the blizzard could hit anytime. The black-and-white paint might survive out here alone tonight, but then again, he might not. Meanwhile everyone at the Last Chance Ranch was gearing up for a festive holiday. Tucker knew all about ruined Christmas celebrations and was determined to save both the stallion and the day.

As a recent hire who didn't much care about Christmas, Tucker had volunteered to get all the Last Chance horses, including Houdini, into their stalls around noon in anticipation of the blizzard. He'd gone back to check on them at about 3:00 p.m. and had come nose-to-nose with Houdini, who'd let himself out of his stall.

Tucker had grabbed for the horse's halter and missed

as Houdini bolted through the open barn door. After making a quick call on his cell to the main house, Tucker had stuffed a sack of oats and a lead rope in the saddlebag of one of the ranch snowmobiles and headed off in pursuit of the stallion.

He cussed out the horse, but mostly he blamed himself. He should have anticipated the jail break, considering the stallion had done it before. Thank God he hadn't unlatched any of the other stalls, which was another one of his tricks.

Houdini could potentially earn thousands in stud fees for the Last Chance provided he didn't freeze his ass out here tonight. Jack Chance, who—along with his two brothers, Nick and Gabe, and his widowed mother, Sarah—owned the Jackson Hole area ranch, had bought the two-year-old for a song because Houdini was untrained and rambunctious. The horse's previous owner had meant to school him, but those plans had been sidetracked by various personal issues.

In the few weeks Houdini had spent at the Last Chance, he'd learned to tolerate a halter and a lead rope, but he had a long way to go before he could be used as a stud, let alone for cutting-horse competitions. His natural curiosity and inventiveness made him a royal pain to deal with.

Tucker felt a certain kinship with the rowdy horse. He hadn't exactly been a model of responsible behavior, either. He'd partied all through high school and had seen no reason to stop doing that after graduation ten years ago. He'd worked just enough to stay solvent.

It was a dead-end street, and when Jack Chance had hired him back in September, they'd discussed Tucker's lack of focus. Tucker had promised he was ready to buckle down and make something of himself. Accidentally allowing Houdini to escape might be a forgivable offense, but Tucker didn't feel that he had room to make mistakes. Retrieving the horse was his job.

Because he'd grown up in the area, he knew that the Last Chance prided itself on offering people and animals a fresh start. He and Houdini had come to the right place. Tucker appreciated that fact, but obviously the horse, after being allowed to do as he pleased for two years, did not.

At least his trail was easy to follow in the fallen snow. That wouldn't be true in a blizzard, however, and flakes had begun swirling through the frigid air. Tucker's sheepskin coat wasn't enough protection from this kind of weather, even with the collar turned up.

He crammed his Stetson on tight and reached up to anchor it with a gloved hand whenever it threatened to blow off. He wished he'd picked up some goggles, but he'd been too intent on rescuing the horse to think of his own comfort. The moisture from his eyes turned his lashes to icicles, but that couldn't be helped.

Thank God the horse had stayed out in the open instead of running into the trees. Tucker needed to catch him before he changed his mind about that, because the snowmobile would be no use in the forested part of Chance land.

Pointing the snowmobile toward a small rise, Tucker hoped to get a glimpse of the horse. Sure enough, the paint galloped merrily through the meadow about two hundred yards ahead of him. The snow was deep enough to spray in all directions, but not deep enough to be dangerous and cause injuries. Houdini seemed to be having the time of his life.

Tucker stopped the snowmobile and gave a sharp whistle, knowing that was probably a waste of breath.

True to form, Houdini didn't break stride. Fogging the air with some choice words, Tucker took off after him.

If the stakes hadn't been so high, Tucker would have enjoyed this chase. Houdini was the picture of carefree pleasure, his tail a white flag signaling his delight at escaping the barn. Tucker understood the urge to throw off the traces. He'd done it often enough.

But reckless behavior had consequences. After one too many drinks last summer, he'd ended up wrecking his truck. Only dumb luck had kept him from injuring or killing someone, and that wreck and subsequent DUI had been a wake-up call.

He'd always admired the Chance brothers—going to work for them represented progress in his mind. He wanted their respect, and letting a valuable stallion escape was a step in the wrong direction. Recapturing Houdini was critical for the horse, but also for Tucker's self-confidence.

Now that he had the stallion in his sights, he felt better about the likelihood of catching him. Getting back might be a little tricky, though. Snow fell more rapidly with every second. It blocked most of the light and at times obscured his view of the racing horse.

Once he had the horse, he'd call the ranch and let them know his status. Ahead of them, a barbed-wire fence came into view, which meant they'd traveled farther than he'd thought and were at the boundary of Chance land. He'd never ridden in this direction before.

That fence could be a huge problem. Houdini could jump it if he took a notion, and the snowmobile… couldn't. "Don't jump the damn fence," Tucker muttered under his breath. "Please."

Houdini galloped toward it as if he had every intention of doing that. Beyond the fence stood a small log cabin with lights on and a ribbon of smoke rising from the chimney. If they had a snowmobile parked in the outbuilding, he'd ask to borrow it if he had to.

But he'd rather capture the horse on this side of the fence and be done with it. He pushed the snowmobile faster, determined to reach Houdini before the horse made it to the fence. He concentrated so hard on that goal that he didn't notice a large rock jutting out of the snow until the snowmobile's runner found it.

Next thing he knew, he lay flat on his back in the snow, the wind knocked clean out of him. The blood roared in his ears as he struggled to breathe. What a fine mess. Houdini was probably over the fence and half a mile away by now. The snowmobile was silent, probably wrecked.

Then a black-and-white muzzle appeared above him. A blast of steamy air hit his face as Houdini snorted.

Relief flooded through Tucker as he grabbed the horse's halter. "Gotcha."

LACEY EVANS HAD HEARD the approaching snowmobile and hoped it wouldn't be anyone coming to check on her. She was doing fine out here by herself, thank you very much. The cabin was filled with the aroma of stew simmering, bread baking and a fire crackling.

The cabin's owner had seemed nervous about renting to her after she'd explained that her male companion wouldn't be joining her as planned. She'd finally convinced the owner that her Forest Service job made her more qualified than most men to spend a few days alone in an isolated cabin. And that definitely included her piece-of-crap ex-boyfriend Lenny.

Going to the window, she peered through the falling snow and figured out that a cowboy on a snowmobile was chasing a horse on the far side of the barbed-wire fence. One of the Chance boys' paints had apparently escaped. She watched the chase with interest.

But when the snowmobile flipped, she shoved her feet into her boots, pulled a stocking cap over her head and snatched up her coat. That cowboy could be in trouble.

Thank goodness he didn't seem to be badly hurt. By the time she reached the fence, he was on his feet and had somehow captured the horse. The snowmobile didn't look particularly good, though. It had landed upside down, and one runner was bent all to hell.

She took the time to put on her insulated gloves. "Are you okay?" she called out.

"I'm fine." His voice was tight with strain. "I... whoa, boy. Whoa!" The horse whinnied and tried to rear, but the cowboy hung on with both gloved hands and brought the horse's head back down.

She admired his determination to keep a grip on the horse, which looked like the devil's own mount as it blew steam from its nostrils and pawed at the ground. "Should I call somebody?"

"That's okay. I have my cell." He looked from the horse to the snowmobile and back at her. "But he's a handful. It'd be a help if you could fetch the lead rope out of the snowmobile's saddlebag. He usually settles down once he's on the lead."

"I can do that." She'd also pick up his hat, which was lying in the snow. She knew how cowboys felt about their hats.

Parting the barbed wire carefully, she leaned down and stepped between the strands. "Will he try to kick me?"

"No." The cowboy gulped in air. "He's not mean.

Just likes to be in control. I'll feel better once I have a lead rope on him."

Lacey retrieved the fallen hat before crouching down and pulling the rope out of the saddlebag. "And then what?"

"I...don't know." The snow fell faster and he muttered under his breath.

She could guess the nature of those mutterings as she handed him the rope and his hat. Anyone from this area knew that Wyoming blizzards could be deadly.

She thought he was local because he looked vaguely familiar. He wasn't a Chance, though. She'd grown up here and knew what each of the Chance men looked like. Still, something about this cowboy was familiar. She'd seen those green eyes and dark hair before.

"Thanks." He put on his hat and clipped the rope to the horse's halter as the snow swirled and gusted around them.

"I hope you're not thinking of riding back."

He greeted that with a short laugh. "He's never been ridden."

"You can wait it out in my cabin, but that doesn't solve the horse issue."

He glanced from the horse to her cabin. "What's in the outbuilding?"

"My Jeep." She raised her voice to be heard over the howl of the wind. "But we can't risk driving in this."

"I know." He secured his hat with one gloved hand when it started to blow off. "But can we stable him there for the night?"

"I guess." She considered the logistics of getting through the fence. "You got wire cutters?"

"Nope."

"Then I'll get mine."

"You have wire cutters?"

"I work for the Forest Service." She started to walk away and turned back as curiosity got the better of her. "Do I know you from somewhere?"

"I grew up here. The name's Tucker Rankin."

"Tucker?" Her eyes widened. "I'm Lacey. Lacey Evans. Jackson Hole High School."

"I'll be damned."

"Small world. I'll be back as quick as I can." She hurried toward the fence and ducked through the strands of barbed wire.

Tucker Rankin. She hadn't thought about him in years. Hurrying toward the cabin's outbuilding, she sorted through her recollections of Tucker. He'd been a bad boy back then, too wild for her, although she'd secretly found him very sexy.

But one vivid memory surfaced. She'd gone to the Christmas formal their senior year against her better judgment. But a sweet, nerdy boy had asked her and she hadn't had the heart to turn him down.

Normally she just didn't do Christmas. Her mother had died when she was fifteen, and her mom had been the person who'd made the holiday special. After that it had been less painful to ignore Christmas completely.

Her dad had remarried when she was seventeen, and although Lacey had tried valiantly to appreciate her stepmother's efforts, the lady wasn't the most sensitive person in the world. She'd crudely trampled on all Lacey's mother's traditions.

A pre-lit artificial tree and battery-operated candles appeared. Cranberry and popcorn garlands were proclaimed too messy. Gifts were opened Christmas Eve instead of Christmas morning. Any reference to Santa was labeled a childish fantasy.

Lacey's sister and brother had adapted, but Lacey, being the oldest, had the strongest memories of pine-scented boughs, flickering beeswax candles, hand-strung garlands and wrapped packages under the tree on Christmas morning. She'd never made the adjustment. Still, she'd agreed to be Arnold's date for the Christmas formal.

Just her luck, the dance committee had decorated a huge evergreen that filled the gym with its fragrance, and they'd continued the torture by placing beeswax votives around the room. When Lacey had slipped outside, tearful with nostalgia, Tucker had been there, too, enjoying a forbidden cigarette.

He'd offered her his coat, and they'd exchanged views on Christmas. She'd found out that his mom had died on Christmas Eve when he was twelve, which was a way worse situation than hers. He didn't celebrate the holiday anymore, either, but a girl had asked him to the formal.

Turned out she'd done it to make another guy jealous, and her ex had arrived to claim her five minutes ago. Tucker wasn't having a particularly good time at this Christmas event, either. They'd shared their holiday angst, both past and present, that night.

They'd also shared a heated kiss that had scared the living daylights out of her. Rattled by the lust he'd inspired with one kiss, she'd returned his coat and dashed back inside. They'd never talked again.

After taking her wire cutters out of the Jeep, she quickly assessed the interior of the outbuilding that doubled as a garage. A horse would fit in there next to her Jeep, which was old and beat up. A few kicks from a horse's hooves wouldn't be noticed.

Inviting Tucker into her cabin to spend the night

wasn't quite so convenient. She'd planned to spend three days there with Lenny. Until a week ago, BTB (Before The Bimbo), she and Lenny had been practically engaged, and she'd intended to take a stab at celebrating Christmas on a small scale.

A one-bedroom hideaway had seemed adequate for a couple. But she and Tucker were not a couple, and there was only one bed. He was too tall to fit comfortably on the couch, and she hated to make him sleep on the floor when she had no sleeping bag or air mattress.

But the blizzard was upon them and he had to get in out of it. They'd work out the details later. She lowered her head and leaned into the wind as she returned to the fence. Tucker stood like a marble statue beside the horse, and Lacey wondered if he held himself rigid so he wouldn't betray any weakness with an unmanly shiver.

"I called the ranch." His lips looked a little blue and his eyelashes and eyebrows were crusted with snow. "I said I'd wait out the storm here. I explained you were an old high school friend."

"Perfect." She had a little trouble manipulating the wire cutters with her thick gloves on, but she managed to cut both strands and pull them back, creating a decent-size opening. "Let's get going. It's cold out here."

His chuckle became a cough. "I noticed. Oh, wait. There's a sack of oats in the saddlebag. I'll lead Houdini if you'll grab the oats. He'll need something to eat."

"Right." She moved quickly through the opening in the fence and over to the snowmobile, which, at the rate it was snowing, would soon be covered. Oats in hand, she followed Tucker through the fence and across what had been a defined road an hour ago. Soon it would be obliterated, too.

She dashed around both horse and man to open the double doors into the outbuilding. The cold must have had a calming effect on the paint, because he walked into the shelter without protest. Maybe he had realized that it wasn't so much fun being outside in a blizzard.

Lacey gestured to the heater designed to prevent engines from freezing. "This should help keep him warmer, too."

"He'll appreciate that." Tucker brushed the snow from Houdini's back before glancing around the make-shift garage. "Do you think I could use that bucket in the corner to feed him some oats?"

"Don't see why not." She retrieved the bucket and handed it to him, along with the small sack of oats. "Will this be enough?"

"I'll only give him half for now, in case I need to ration it." He opened the sack and poured some into the bucket while managing to hold it away from Houdini. Once he set it down, the horse shoved his nose deep into the bucket and began munching. The bucket rattled against the outbuilding's cement floor.

Lacey couldn't imagine that little bit of oats would satisfy an animal of Houdini's size. "I brought apples, and I have some carrots left over from the stew I made, if you want to give him those later on."

"Stew?" Tucker was so obviously trying to control his shivers as he smiled at her. "God, that s-sounds wonderful."

"You're frozen, aren't you?"

"Pretty much."

"Then let's get inside and warm you up." She'd thought it was an innocent remark, but as they closed the horse inside the outbuilding and she led the way into the cabin, she thought about how she could warm him up, and it had nothing to do with stew.

That kiss had replayed itself in her mind quite a few times since she'd found out who he was. He'd had a reputation in high school as a skilled lover, and if that kiss had been a sample, his reputation had been well deserved. For several months after the kiss, she'd had potent dreams involving naked bodies writhing on soft sheets.

And here she was, snowbound with the object of her teenage fantasies. She blew out an impatient breath. What nonsense. For all she knew Tucker was married and had a couple of kids.

Once they were inside the warm cabin and had started divesting themselves of their jackets and gloves, she glanced at him. "I suppose someone will be really disappointed if you don't show up for Christmas Eve."

He hooked his coat on a peg by the door and followed it with his hat. "Can't say that they will." He turned to gaze at her. "Are you out here by yourself?"

"Yes." So he was single, apparently. "It just turned out that way." She tried not to gawk, but damn, he was even better looking now than he had been in high school. His features were more chiseled, and the hint of a beard gave him a rugged look that stirred up butterflies in her stomach.

His glance swept the cabin's living room and open kitchen. "No holiday decorations, I see."

"Nope." And he smelled good, too—the musky scent of a man who worked with animals. She hadn't realized how much she liked that earthy aroma on a man.

"I'm going to take a wild guess that you're not into this holiday any more than you were years ago when we had that conversation outside the school gym."

"So you remember that." She met his gaze. It wasn't the conversation she was focusing on, but what had followed. The mouth she'd kissed long ago looked much the same except for some added smile lines bracketing his firm lips.

"Yeah, I do remember, in fact." A telltale flicker in his green eyes contradicted his casual tone.

Her heart rate increased another notch. She'd bet money he was thinking about that kiss, too. "Well, you're right. I still don't much like Christmas. How about you?"

"Can't say it's my favorite time of year."

She kept her attention on his face, but she was very aware of the snug fit of his Western shirt. The soft blue plaid revealed muscles honed by ranch work. "I'll bet the Last Chance goes all out."

He rolled his eyes. "You have no idea. Fifteen-foot tree in the living room, holly and pine boughs on the banister going upstairs, red velvet bows on everything that doesn't move. They've even decorated the damned barn."

She ignored a sharp pang of longing. Being surrounded by that kind of festive atmosphere would only make her sad. "You won't find that here."

"Good. Maybe it's just as well we ended up together tonight." He smiled. "We're birds of a feather."

Oh, yeah. She remembered that smile—the one that went from boyish to seductive in zero-point-five seconds. Heat spiraled through her system. Ten years ago she hadn't allowed herself to be swept away by his animal magnetism. But tonight, after being dumped last week by the man she'd thought she'd eventually marry, all bets were off.

2

Lacey Evans. Whenever he'd thought of her in the years since high school, which had been more times than he cared to admit, he'd pictured her with a stodgy but successful husband and a couple of cute kids. Once again she'd be totally out of reach, as she had been when they were in high school.

Instead, against all odds, he was standing in this cozy cabin with her. She didn't seem to be attached to a guy, let alone have any kids. She hadn't known he would show up, so the setting she'd created had nothing to do with him.

But she couldn't have planned a more tempting scenario than a welcoming fire, a home-cooked meal and the prospect of spending time with a woman he'd wanted desperately when he was eighteen. Who needed Christmas?

The years had been good to her. Her honey-colored hair was slightly darker now, and she wore it shorter, too, an easy-care mop of caramel curls. Those curls were tousled by the stocking cap she'd pulled off, and he had the urge to comb her hair into place with his fingers.

Her blue eyes were no longer so wide and endearingly innocent. After she'd run from his kiss that night, her cheeks bright pink, he'd decided that he'd been French-kissing a virgin. But there was nothing virginal in her frank appraisal of him now. The glow in those amazing eyes told him that if he kissed her again, she wouldn't run.

The possibility heated his blood, and suddenly, he wasn't the least bit cold. She'd had that effect on him from the first day he'd glimpsed her walking down the hall at Jackson Hole High, her snug sweater and jeans showing off a sweetly curved figure. He'd thought he'd died and gone to heaven the one and only time he'd held her in his arms.

When she'd ended that unforgettable kiss, she'd returned his coat. He'd left it off in hopes cold air would deflate his penis enough for him to walk to his truck and drive home. The wait had seemed like hours.

He liked to think he had more control these days, but apparently not when it came to Lacey. She still favored snug jeans and close-fitting sweaters. Today's sweater was green, which signaled full speed ahead to his eager package.

Tucker decided, in the name of his own self-respect, to show some restraint. Although he wasn't proud of it, he'd engaged in some meaningless sex over the years. When life was one big party, a guy didn't much care who he slept with if the woman was willing and warm.

But Lacey was different. She wasn't just some girl he'd met in a cowboy bar. Yeah, he wanted her, but he didn't have to act on that urge. Instead, he could distract himself by concentrating on a different kind of hunger.

He glanced over at the stove, the source of mouthwatering aromas. "I don't know much about cooking, but is there any chance that stew is ready to eat?"

She smiled. "Yep. Your timing is excellent."

"Dumb luck." But he'd had quite a bit of luck lately, especially landing the job at the Last Chance. He was beginning to wonder if Houdini's escape had been an example of good luck disguised as potential disaster. "What can I do to help?"

"Not a thing. If you want to wash up, there's soap and towels in the bathroom." She gestured toward a short hall. "First door on your left."

"Thanks. Good plan." He probably smelled of horse. Some women liked that, but he didn't know if Lacey did or not. He headed down the hall, his boots clicking on the hardwood floor of the cabin.

The bathroom was plain—white fixtures and a tub with a white shower curtain. Tucker caught a glimpse of himself in the medicine cabinet mirror and winced. Hat hair, red nose, five-o'clock shadow. He must have imagined that glint of interest in her eyes. What woman would be attracted to *that?*

Rolling back his sleeves, he turned on the water and picked up the soap. He couldn't do anything about the five-o'clock shadow, but soap and warm water would make him feel more presentable. Then he noticed that the soap was embedded with an image of Santa Claus.

The cabin's owners might have left it, but the lack of frills everywhere else made that unlikely. Probably somebody had given it to Lacey and she was practical enough to make use of it. He could help her with that.

He lathered up, scrubbing his face and hands until they tingled. The soap smelled like candy canes. He hadn't thought of those in a while. His mom used to buy a lot of them to decorate the tree because they were affordable.

His dad had thought the whole tree thing was a waste of money, but his mom had insisted on having one every year. She and Tucker had strung popcorn and made chains of construction paper. That had all ended when she died.

No point in dredging up those memories, though, especially when he was with a woman who also ignored the holiday except for some soap she was trying to use up. He splashed cold water on his face, grabbed a towel and dried off. Then he finger-combed his hair as best he could.

He walked back into the kitchen, where a loaf of what looked like homemade bread sat on a cutting board in the middle of the table. Lacey was dishing stew into a couple of generously sized bowls. The light caught in her caramel curls as she glanced up and smiled at him.

His breath stalled at the beauty of the scene, at the beauty of her, all flushed from the heat of the stove. Or maybe her extra color had something to do with him being there. That was a happy prospect.

"This looks wonderful. Thank you." Then he had a thought. "Listen, if you feed me now, are you going to have enough supplies for your stay?"

"Oh, yeah." She laughed as she opened the refrigerator, which was stuffed. "I read the weather reports and decided to be prepared for anything. As I said, I can probably help feed your horse if it comes to that."

"He's not exactly my horse. I just work there. But I'm relieved to know you stocked up."

"The good news is I'm loaded with provisions. The

bad news is the provisions are everything I like, but you may not like the same things."

"Beggars can't be choosers. I'm grateful for whatever you're willing to share."

Her quick glance in his direction told him that she'd taken that in a way he hadn't meant. God, he hoped he hadn't offended her. "Sorry. That didn't come out right."

She became very busy ladling out the stew. "Don't worry about it. I mean, we had that one silly moment together after the winter formal, but I'm not at all your type."

"Why do you say that?"

"It's obvious." She set the bowls down on the table with brisk efficiency. "You went out with the party girls, whereas I was—"

"Too good for me."

"What?" She looked up in obvious surprise.

"You heard me. I was the bad boy with the souped-up truck and mediocre grades. You were an honor student with goals and a curfew."

"Okay, so we were different, but I never thought I was too good for you, Tucker."

"No, you wouldn't think that, because you're a nice person. But I knew it. It didn't stop me from kissing you, though. I saw my opportunity and took advantage of you being sad and vulnerable." He rubbed the back of his neck, where tension had gathered. He hadn't meant to start confessing his sins, but now that he had... "I shouldn't have kissed you that night."

"So you regret it?"

He met her gaze and something in the depths of those blue eyes demanded complete honesty. "No," he said softly. "I'm not that noble."

"Well, that's a relief." The corners of her mouth turned up in a saucy smile.

He stared at her. He still hadn't quite made the adjustment from the virginal Lacey to the more self-assured woman standing in front of him. Once he did, he'd have a helluva time keeping his hands to himself.

She gestured toward the table as if ready to change the subject. "As I was saying, the supplies are all things I like. That means your choice of beverage is coffee, water, or wine. Most cowboys I know prefer beer."

He was more than ready to change the subject. Although he did prefer beer, he'd been known to drink wine. But he wasn't going to use up whatever she'd brought for herself. That would be rude. "I'll just drink water."

"You're sure? I'm having wine and unless you hate it, you're welcome to have some with me."

"I don't hate it, but I wouldn't feel right using up your—"

"Oh, for heaven's sake." She pulled two goblets out of the cupboard and set one by each plate. "Besides, I think we need to toast."

"To Christmas?" He had a tough time believing she'd want to do that.

"No, to meeting again after all these years."

"Oh." He was flattered that she'd count it a toasting occasion. "I guess we could toast to that."

"It's quite a coincidence, don't you think?"

"I do. It took a runaway horse and a wrecked snowmobile to accomplish it."

She opened the wine and poured each of them a glass. "And a slimeball. Let's not forget my worthless ex."

"Husband?" His high spirits plummeted. He should

have known she hadn't intended to be out here all by herself, that a man had originally been part of the deal.

"Boyfriend." She picked up her wineglass and handed one to him. "Fortunately that's all he ever was."

Tucker understood now why she'd looked at him with interest. With his playboy reputation, he had a history of attracting women on the rebound. That kind of relationship wasn't built to last. Either the woman moved on after she felt better about herself or she went back to her ex.

Usually that was fine with him, because he was careful not to get invested. But he didn't feel like being Lacey's rebound guy. She held a special place in his heart, and he didn't want to tarnish that memory.

Still, he knew his lines in situations like this. "Your ex is obviously a loser if he let you go."

"Thank you. I agree." She lifted her glass. "To old friends."

"To old friends." He touched his glass to hers and drank. But as he lowered the glass, honesty made him speak up. "We weren't really friends in high school, Lacey."

"Depends on how you define it. I thought we became friends that night outside the gym."

"I guess." If she hadn't run away, they would have become more than friends. He was glad they hadn't. He'd have enough trouble keeping this night from veering toward sex when all he'd done was kiss her. If she hadn't left, he would have continued the seduction he'd begun with that kiss. He'd been eighteen and flooded with hormones.

Now he was twenty-eight, and still somewhat hormone driven, but not to the exclusion of all reason. When necessary he could summon a little common sense. Lacey was a woman he could fall for, and yet she'd been recently dumped. That combo meant she was off limits.

She waved a hand at the table. "Let's eat."

"Good idea." Tucker hadn't been particularly polished when he'd arrived at the Last Chance, but Sarah Chance was a stickler for good manners. He'd learned that any cowboy who worked at the ranch had better know the fundamentals or risk losing his job.

Setting down his wineglass, he rounded the table to pull out Lacey's chair.

"How gallant." She accepted the gesture with a smile and slipped gracefully into the chair.

As he scooted it forward, he breathed in the scent of candy canes and woman. Obviously she'd used that soap, too. He wanted to bury his nose in the curve of her neck and nibble on her earlobe. But that wouldn't be wise.

He took a seat opposite her, unfolded the paper napkin she'd provided and settled it on his lap. Outside, the wind rattled the windowpanes, which made their dinner seem all the more cozy in comparison. The food smelled delicious, but hungry as he was, he waited for Lacey to start eating.

She began by picking up a serrated knife and slicing off a couple pieces of bread. The scent of it burst forth, beckoning him with an aroma that reminded him of good sex. He'd always thought food and lovemaking went together.

He set that notion firmly aside. "I didn't know you could cook."

"You still don't." She held out the breadboard. "For all you know, this tastes like Styrofoam."

He picked up the heel, bit into its soft center, and closed his eyes. Heaven.

"It must be all right."

"Mmm." He glanced at her and nodded enthusiastically as he chewed.

"Fortunately my mom taught me to bake when I was a kid. I picked up basic cooking skills when I realized my dad was hopeless in the kitchen. Of course, now he has Helen."

Grasping at a subject that didn't involve naked bodies, he asked about her family as they both dug into the beef stew.

She chose to ignore her dad and Helen and talk about her siblings, instead. Kathy, four years younger than she was, had married and moved to Ohio. Steven was finishing a degree in engineering at the University of Wyoming. Even given Lacey's reluctance to celebrate Christmas, Tucker was surprised she wasn't with her family right now, and he said as much.

"I know it's not very evolved of me, but I grit my teeth whenever I have to watch the way Helen celebrates Christmas," she said. "So I keep my participation to a minimum. This year I used Lenny as an excuse. I told them he was likely to propose over the holiday, and that I thought the two of us should create our own special memories by renting this cute little cabin for a week during Christmas."

"Do they know Lenny's not here with you?"

"No. I decided when he bailed that I'd keep that info to myself and come out here alone. The irony is that I really had planned to have a semi-normal Christmas with him. He likes the holiday, so I was going to make an effort for his sake, sort of to prove I could."

Tucker put down his spoon. "What happened with

Lenny?" He cared about her broken heart and was willing to let her talk it out. That didn't mean he had to make it all better with some good sex, though. There was such a thing as self-preservation.

"Two weeks ago he met somebody he liked better, somebody who didn't have—to use his phrase—my baggage."

Tucker had the immediate urge to clean the guy's clock. "Hell, everyone has baggage."

"I know." She sliced off two more pieces of bread and gestured for him to take one. "Maybe Lenny and his girlfriend, Suzanne, have matching luggage tags."

"Could be, but I'll bet they're attached to the most boring suitcases in the world, that black nylon kind a million other people have."

She smiled at him. "I like to think so."

"Whereas yours has style. It might even be purple."

That made her laugh. "Okay, that's my new slogan. *I may have baggage, but I carry it with style.*"

"You do, Lacey." He picked up his wineglass and lifted it in her direction. The sparkle was back in her blue eyes, and he liked seeing that. "You definitely do."

"Thanks, Tucker." She lifted her glass, too. "So do you."

She wouldn't think so if she knew what a screwup he'd been recently. He wished now that he'd made more of himself in the years since they'd last met. She'd probably earned a degree before landing her Forest Service job.

Then something occurred to him. "Did you go into forestry because of the trees?" Once the words were out of his mouth, he realized how stupid that sounded. Didn't everybody who majored in forestry love trees?

"I mean, because you used to love the evergreens at Christmas time."

She paused, a spoonful of stew halfway to her mouth, and stared at him. "You are the only person who's made that connection. I didn't realize it myself until recently, when I started thinking about celebrating a real Christmas here with Lenny and knew I'd want a real tree."

"But you gave up the idea when he…" He wasn't sure what term to use that wouldn't be insulting.

"When he dumped me. You can say it. It's the truth, after all. And a girl who's been dumped right before Christmas usually isn't ready to deck the halls with boughs of holly, if you get my drift." She continued eating her stew.

"Maybe that's exactly the time to do it."

She stopped eating and gazed at him. "How so?"

"You were going to celebrate Christmas for Lenny's sake, right?"

"Yeah, but obviously I picked the wrong guy to jump-start my Christmas spirit. He's pushed me right back into bah-humbug territory."

Tucker recognized that kind of thinking. For years he'd seen himself as a victim of circumstance. Hearing it coming from Lacey was unsettling. Funny how much easier it was to figure out what other people should do to make themselves happy.

"Tucker, why are you looking at me like that?"

"I'm just wondering why you'd break out the decorations for a guy, but not for yourself. Why let his dumb decisions keep you from celebrating if you have the urge to do it?"

She frowned. "I'm not saying I wanted to, but I

thought it was time to see if I could, because depriving him of the holiday wasn't fair."

"Is it fair to deprive yourself? When we talked outside the gym, I got the impression that you used to love Christmas, especially the way your mother celebrated it." And so had he. His words were as much directed at himself as at her.

Her expression softened. "I did love it back then, but I can't re-create that kind of Christmas because my mom was such a huge part of it, and she's gone. I thought maybe I'd try for some new traditions with Lenny, but bravely forging my own rituals without anyone to share them seems a little desperate and pathetic."

"I get that. I've thought exactly the same thing, so in the past I've spent Christmas Eve in a bar, which is desperate and pathetic in its own way."

"I usually plan a trip somewhere tropical." She shrugged. "It sort of works."

He had a sudden image of Lacey in a bikini sipping an umbrella drink. He shoved that image away immediately. "That's classier than my option."

"Last Christmas I talked Lenny into flying to Bermuda, but he hated that it didn't feel like Christmas. I still wasn't ready to spend the holiday at his family's house or mine, so this was the compromise."

Tucker blew out a breath. "I'm sorry it all fell apart, Lacey. He's an impatient creep who doesn't know what he's lost."

"To be honest, I was having doubts about the relationship. We weren't clicking the way I thought a committed couple should. Spending Christmas here was going to be a kind of test." She grimaced. "Guess it was, at that."

"You're way better off. You deserve somebody special." Any guy who rejected such a wonderful woman was terminally stupid.

"Thanks." Once again her eyes took on a happy gleam.

He hoped his next suggestion wouldn't bring back the shadows that had lurked in her gaze earlier. He cleared his throat. "Anyway, we're stuck together for at least tonight, and we understand each other's take on Christmas. I'm thinking it's the perfect chance to get over ourselves and celebrate the damned holiday."

3

"CELEBRATE CHRISTMAS?" Lacey couldn't believe he'd said that. Of all the people in the world, Tucker seemed the least likely to suggest such a thing. "We can't."

"Why not?"

"I didn't bring any decorations, for one thing. I had planned to, but when Lenny bailed, I donated all the stuff I'd bought to the Salvation Army."

"Except the soap."

She rolled her eyes. "Ah, yes, the soap. It was a secret Santa thing at work, and I happened to be out of soap, so I brought it on this trip instead of throwing it in the Salvation Army donation bag. Are you suggesting we prop the soap on the mantel and call it good?"

He grinned at her. "It's a start."

That grin was lethal. She didn't really want to decorate for Christmas, but if he did, she was willing to go along just on the basis of that killer smile. He also had a point about celebrating with someone who understood the issues. She wouldn't have to fake anything with Tucker.

"I have some emergency candles in case the power

goes out," she said. "We could put one on each side of the soap."

He nodded. "See how this plan is taking shape already?"

"Oh, yeah. We'll rival Rockefeller Center in no time."

"Don't make fun. Santa soap and candles could look really nice on the mantel, even if the candles aren't beeswax, which I'm guessing they're not."

"Nope. Just those cheap white paraffin kind." She gazed at him, marveling that he'd remembered a detail like beeswax candles. "So you really were listening when we had that conversation."

"Of course. Got any popcorn?"

"A couple of bags of the microwave kind, but—"

"Needle and thread?"

"Some. I carry a little sewing kit in my cosmetic bag, but—"

He pushed back his chair. "Then let's get popping. It needs to cool before we string it."

"Tucker, we don't have a tree."

"Don't worry." His green gaze found hers. "We will." Then he walked over and took his coat and hat off the peg where it was hanging by the front door.

"Wait a minute." She stood and followed him. "You can't go out there and cut down a tree. I'm renting this place. The landlord would have a fit."

"I'm not going to cut it down." He settled his hat on his head. "I'll dig it up. Then we can put it back in the ground later. No one has to know."

"The ground's frozen."

"Most places, yes, but on the sunny side of the cabin, it might not be as hard." He shoved his arms into the sleeves of his sheepskin coat.

"But there's a blizzard going on!" As if to emphasize the fact, the wind howled down the chimney and made the fire gyrate wildly.

"That makes it more exciting." He dazzled her with another smile. That, combined with the shadow of a beard, made him look rakish and slightly dangerous.

"You're crazy." Breathing quickly, both from the zing of attraction and her determination to stop him, she backed against the door, arms spread. "I won't let you go out there."

He winked, the picture of male assurance. "Yeah, you will. We're going to do this."

"No, we aren't. People get lost and die in snowstorms, sometimes when they're within a few feet of shelter because they get lost in all that whiteness."

He buttoned up his coat. "I know that. I promise to stay close enough to the cabin and the outbuilding that I can still see them."

"You could get distracted looking for a tree to dig up."

"I could, but I won't. By the way, do you have a shovel in your Jeep?"

"I'm not going to tell you."

"Which means yes."

"Doesn't matter." She remained planted firmly in front of the door. "I'm not moving."

His gaze reflected amusement as it swept over her. "I should warn you that once I get an idea in my head, I can't let it go."

"You'll have to let this one go." She lifted her chin in defiance. "I've been involved in too many search and rescue missions to allow you to take the chance of freezing to death out there. I'd given you more credit for good sense."

"There's your first mistake." And without warning, he leaned in and kissed her.

Her gasp of surprise allowed him to deepen the kiss, which quickly evolved into something spectacular. Bracing both hands against the door beside her head, he angled his mouth over hers and pressed in deep. The sweet invasion made her forget whatever silly argument they'd been having.

As his lips moved against hers in slow seduction, as his tongue explored with lazy intent, her senses rocketed back to the night of the Christmas formal. Yes, this was how she remembered his kiss—a take-no-prisoners assault that reduced her to a ragdoll willing to surrender to whatever he wanted.

She clutched his shoulders as the room seemed to spin. When he lifted his head to smile down at her, she realized the room hadn't been spinning, but she had. He'd circled her waist with both hands and turned her around so that she no longer blocked the door. She'd been so immersed in his kiss that she hadn't noticed.

"I promise not to get lost in the snow," he said. Then he released her and was out the door before she could frame a response.

"You don't fight fair!" she called after him when she managed to catch her breath.

The door opened a crack. "Nuke the popcorn!" Then he closed the door and was gone.

Grabbing the doorknob, she pulled the door open. A blast of frigid air filled with wet snow hit her in the face. "Use the rope!" She hurled the command out into the bitter cold where she could barely see him, head down, burrowing into the storm like a linebacker. "There's a long rope in the Jeep!"

"Thanks!" His answer was faint, but at least he'd heard and acknowledged her order.

She closed the door and stood there shivering, her arms wrapped protectively around her body. He was nuts, crazy as a loon. What kind of man risked his safety to bring a Christmas tree to a woman who didn't want to celebrate in the first place?

Yet she sensed that this wasn't all about her. In helping to slay her demons, he was also facing down his own. She couldn't very well deny him the chance to do that, and if he used the rope, tying it to the latch on the outbuilding and then around his waist, he would have a lifeline back to safety.

The rope was part of her search and rescue gear, but it would serve the purpose of orienting Tucker while he tried to locate a tree. People who lived in this part of the country often tied rope lines between the house and the barn so they'd have something to guide them when they checked on the animals during a snowstorm. Knowing Tucker would use that rope made her feel marginally better about him taking on this job.

He'd been a reckless kid in high school, and so far he'd confirmed that he still possessed that trait. Taking a snowmobile into the teeth of a storm to chase a runaway horse might be brave, but it was also foolish. If the horse had run in a different direction, away from all habitation… She didn't like to think how that might have turned out.

And yet, his reckless nature was part of what made him so sexy. When he'd impulsively kissed her, mostly to get his own way about the tree, she'd tasted a kind of thrilling abandon that didn't come her way often. In fact, she hadn't encountered it since the night of the Christmas formal.

Was that kiss simply a means to an end, getting past her objections to his plan? Or would he take it a step further when he returned? Then again, maybe he'd wait for her to make the next move.

Now that he was outside, she had a chance to think more clearly about what might or might not happen between them tonight. She should decide what she wanted now instead of making that decision in the heat of the moment. As she'd just discovered, a moment with Tucker could get very hot very fast.

Oh, who was she kidding? There was no decision to be made here. Her fantasy man had appeared on her doorstep when neither of them was committed to someone else. If she ever intended to discover what making love to Tucker was all about, now was the time.

And that prospect set her panties on fire. She hurried into the bathroom and rummaged through her cosmetic case to see if...yes! She still had the box of condoms she'd become accustomed to taking along on trips with Lenny. He never seemed to remember, which should have been another sign that he was the wrong guy. The right guy wouldn't leave that responsibility up to the woman in his life.

She tucked the box back into the case and closed the lid. Her heart was beating so fast she pressed a hand to her chest and took a shaky breath. She had the man, and she had the condoms. This could be the best Christmas Eve of her entire life.

AS NEEDLES OF SNOW HIT his cheeks and the wind threatened to blow him over on his way to the outbuilding, Tucker considered the fact that Lacey might be right. He very well could be crazy for coming out here to dig up a tree. Back in the cabin he'd pictured himself as a

valiant hero who braved the storm to bring her an evergreen on Christmas Eve.

But when a guy made a boast like that, he had to
produce or come off as a braggart who couldn't follow
through. The possibility of staggering back into the
cabin, treeless and frozen, hadn't occurred to him when
he'd left. It sure as hell occurred to him now that he was
in a pitched battle with the wind and snow.

Adding to his idiocy was his most recent move—
kissing Lacey. He really shouldn't have done that, but
kissing her had seemed like a better option than standing there arguing with her. He'd known it would distract her.

Maybe, somewhere in his pea brain, he'd hoped she
wouldn't kiss the way he remembered, which would
help him put the brakes on his lust. But no. If anything,
his memory hadn't done justice to the experience of
going mouth-to-mouth with Lacey.

He thought again of Lenny and couldn't imagine
how anyone could give up kisses like that. Maybe she
didn't kiss Lenny the same way. Maybe Tucker brought
out her inner wild woman.

Yeah, right. That kind of thinking was exactly what
got him into trouble every damned time. He'd decide
that the woman in question had never had someone love
her right, and it was up to him, Supercock, to give her
the kind of pleasure she deserved. He needed to forget
that crap.

At the moment, he had one heroic job, and that involved digging up a Christmas tree. That should cool
his jets for the time being. The storm was a humdinger.

Luckily he was moving into the wind, which pushed
his hat onto his head. But on the way back he'd be in
danger of losing it, especially if and when he dug up a

tree and had to wrangle that back to the cabin. He was definitely nuts for doing this.

Well, maybe not entirely. He and Lacey really did need to get over their holiday issues. Speaking for himself, the idea of making Christmas happen for the first time since his mom died held a certain appeal. He'd never been moved to do it for anyone else, but he was obviously a sucker for Lacey. Sharing a Christmas celebration with her seemed like the right thing to do on many counts.

But first he had to come up with the tree. And get into the damned outbuilding when snow had piled up against a door that was probably frozen shut by now. He kicked most of the snow away and pried open the latch.

This had sounded so easy when he'd described it to Lacey. Putting his whole weight behind the effort, he finally wrenched open the door with a loud crack. Instantly he positioned himself in the opening in case Houdini stood right there, ready to make a run for it. When no Houdini nose shoved against his chest, he slipped inside quickly and reached for the light switch as he pulled the door closed.

Houdini dozed peacefully in his allotted space next to the Jeep. Apparently the horse had worn himself out running through the snow earlier. Bonus. The Jeep looked okay, but some fresh chew marks on a two-by-four stud were probably Houdini's handiwork. Tucker decided not to worry about that now. He'd assess the damage after the storm ended.

Relieved that Houdini seemed to be settled into his temporary quarters just fine, Tucker rummaged in the back of the Jeep and located both a shovel and the hefty coil of rope. He also needed something for the tree's root ball, but the only bucket turned out to be the one he'd used for Houdini's oats. He'd need that again.

On a shelf near the door, he found an empty burlap sack and took that, instead. The outbuilding felt cozy, but Tucker didn't linger. He had a tree to dig up.

Once he was back outside in the bone-chilling cold, he secured the outbuilding's double doors and tied one end of the rope to the latch. He wrapped the other end around his waist and knotted it, although his dexterity was hampered by the freezing temperature and the shovel and sack he held.

Finally he was armed and ready to bag himself a tree. Failure was not an option.

He took a moment to orient himself and walked around to the back side of the cabin, which faced south and was the most likely to have unfrozen ground. He trailed Lacey's rope behind him. Although he'd initially imagined hauling in a man-size blue spruce, he'd scaled back his expectations to a child-size pine. In some things, size mattered. In this case, it was the thought that counted.

But he didn't have a lot of choices. Exactly one tree grew next to the cabin in what might be unfrozen ground. The tree had a nice shape, but it stood at least seven feet tall. Tucker surveyed the situation, took note of the condition of his fingers, toes and nose, and decided digging up this very tree was the best he could hope for.

Some time later—could have been thirty minutes, could have been an hour, could have been two hours— he enclosed the tree's roots in the burlap sack and half carried, half dragged the tree around to the front of the cabin and up the steps to the small porch. She'd better love it, that was all he could say. He would have thought all that effort would warm him up, but instead he was one gigantic icicle.

As if she'd been listening for his approach, she threw open the door. "At last! I was ready to send out the St. Bernard with a keg of whiskey!"

"Took longer than I thought."

Her attention strayed to the tree lying on the porch. "Oh, Tucker. It's perfect." She stepped back so he could wrestle the tree inside. "Plus it smells *wonderful*."

He'd have to take her word for it. His nostrils were frozen shut. He'd been mouth-breathing for what seemed like hours.

"I cleared a place for it in the corner."

Branches scraped along the hardwood floor and he hoped the tree wasn't leaking sap. Then he realized that nothing would be leaking sap, including him, when the outside temperature was this cold. All gelatinous substances would be solids by now.

He'd dug up as much of the root system as he had the energy for. Consequently, the tree had a solid base of roots and soil inside the burlap. Once he tipped the tree upright, it stood straight and looked magnificent, exactly as he'd pictured it would.

"Tucker, that's amazing."

He glanced over and discovered her gratitude and awe was directed at him, not the tree. He'd impressed her, and suddenly the ordeal was worth every finger-numbing, toe-numbing second he'd endured.

Feeling like Paul Bunyan, he stood back and admired his work. "Now *that's* a Christmas tree."

"Yes, it most definitely is."

Next he tried to unbutton his coat, which was a chore because he couldn't feel his fingers and had forgotten he was still wearing gloves.

"Here, let me help you with that." Moving in front of him, she gently pulled off his gloves and dropped them to the floor.

His fingers began to tingle as the numbness disappeared. He flexed them and decided he'd been through worse.

Then she began unfastening the buttons on his coat, which were covered with snow.

He let his arms drop to his sides and watched her intently pursuing her goal. If he wasn't so damned cold, this would be erotic. Good thing he was frozen, because now that he'd brought home the trophy tree, he had the unwise urge to claim his reward.

Fortunately his penis wouldn't be up to claiming anything until he'd thawed out some. Even then, he had another sizable issue that would keep his bad boy in check. Thank God he was totally condomless. The heady feeling of being admired and fussed over for his tree-bagging abilities was making mincemeat of his vow not to get physical with her.

"You're really shaking, Tucker. I'm worried that you're suffering from mild hypothermia." She peeled off his coat and dropped it on the floor.

He doubted that. He'd been dealing with this kind of weather all his life, and he'd never had a problem with it. But he was human, and having her fret over his well-being felt nice, so he kept his mouth shut.

"Sit down on the couch. I'll take off your boots."

He complied.

She pulled off his boots with brisk efficiency and then removed his wool socks. "God, your feet are like ice."

He didn't know if they were or not. He couldn't feel them yet.

"Come with me." She grasped his hand, which was still prickling, and urged him to his feet. "What you need is to get out of these clothes and into a warm bed."

He couldn't recall ever refusing a beautiful woman's invitation to get into her bed, but he had to refuse this time. "That's okay. I'll be fine here by the fire."

"Look, this isn't up for debate. I'm not about to have you put your health at risk because of this daring tree project. It was a wonderful gesture, and I want you to be well enough to enjoy it." She tugged harder. "Now, come on. Don't make me get nasty."

He had to admit that crawling into a warm bed sounded terrific, at least until he warmed up. She hadn't said she'd get in there with him, so maybe it would be okay. Once he wasn't shivering so much, he'd get dressed again and they'd decorate the tree together.

"Okay. Just for a few minutes." He allowed himself to be led into the bedroom. Nothing would happen there. Without condoms, nothing *could* happen there. End of story.

4

LACEY WASN'T ABOUT TO let Tucker's heroic Christmas tree project put him at risk. The fact that he was shaking was a good sign and meant his body was still trying to warm itself. But he'd been out there nearly an hour, and she wasn't taking any chances considering how isolated they were.

She'd put him to bed and brew him some tea. Anyone who'd dealt with hypothermia would do the same. The fact that he was six-foot-plus of dark-haired, green-eyed yumminess wasn't the dominant factor, here.

But it was *a* factor. She threw back the covers on the cabin's queen-size bed before turning to him. Her gaze traveled from his broad shoulders to his narrow hips, and she swallowed. Taking off his gloves and coat were one thing. Removing the rest of his clothes was quite another.

She glanced into his eyes, which seemed somewhat unfocused. "Do you think you can undress yourself?"

His teeth chattered as he continued to shiver. "Sure. Go on back by the f-fire. I'll b-be fine." He fumbled with the snaps on his shirt.

"Never mind." She nudged his hands away. "It'll go faster if I do it." Taking a deep breath, she tackled the snaps. The material was cold, but she was encouraged by the warmth of his body underneath. He was still quivering, but at least his skin wasn't clammy. "I think you're going to be okay. This is just a precaution."

He nodded as he stood meekly letting her unfasten the snaps at his wrists and pull the shirt from his waistband. Once she'd tossed the shirt on the floor, she worked his T-shirt off. He leaned down slightly so she could pull it over his head.

At that point her objectivity began to slip. She forced herself to ignore the breadth of his chest, the dark hair sprinkled over it, and the intoxicating scent of his skin. She reminded herself that hypothermia was serious, a condition not to be messed with.

Keeping that thought foremost in her mind, she reached for his belt buckle. But as she did, his hand closed over hers.

"That's good enough," he said. "You can stop, now."

She glanced up and met a gaze so hot she nearly went up in flames.

"I don't need to crawl into that bed, after all." His voice was husky. "If you'll just go on out to the living room and wait for me, I'll be there in a few minutes."

Her heart raced and moisture gathered between her thighs. It didn't take a genius to figure out that she'd aroused him with the undressing routine. Standing here by the bed presented the ideal opportunity to do something about that. She admitted the possibility of sex with him had been in the back of her mind, assuming he really didn't have hypothermia.

And yet Tucker acted as if he didn't intend to take advantage of the situation she'd created for them. Given his reputation and his obvious attraction to her, she had to believe he wanted to. Lack of birth control had to be the thing stopping him.

So now what? Should she announce that she had a box of condoms? That seemed sort of…tacky. But if she didn't let him know about them, he would continue to avoid any possibility of having sex with her tonight. That would be a waste for both of them.

"I mean it, Lacey. You need to leave."

She kept looking into his eyes because they were begging her to stay even though his words told her to go. She swallowed. "What—what if I don't want to leave?"

He groaned. "It's best if you do."

"What would you say if I told you I have…condoms?"

His eyes widened.

"I was always in charge of bringing them, and I forgot to take them out of my travel case for this trip."

"You were always in charge of condoms? What kind of man expects that of a woman?"

"The same kind who dumps her right before Christmas, I guess. Anyway, I have them."

He blew out a breath. "Right."

Oh, God. The issue wasn't condoms. Or if it was, he was put off by the idea of using some bought for another man. What she'd thought was a happy accident might be a colossal insult.

How awkward was this? Her face hot with embarrassment, she looked away. "Never mind," she murmured. "Forget I said anything. I'll see you in the living room." She started to leave.

"Wait." He caught her arm.

"Listen, Tucker, I'm sure your instincts are on target." She still didn't look at him.

"Or maybe yours are." He pulled her gently back until she was facing him. "Just so you know, I want you desperately."

"Yes, but you have misgivings."

His smile was soft. "Not anymore." And then he kissed her with such thoroughness that she believed him.

He continued to kiss her until her resistance disappeared and her body grew molten with desire. Soon nothing was more important than making love with Tucker. And even though he had a reputation for making any woman he touched feel that way, she knew that for this moment, she was the only one who mattered to him. That was enough.

At last he released her and brushed his thumb slowly over her well-kissed mouth. "The condoms are where?"

"Finish getting out of your clothes." She moved reluctantly from the warmth of his arms and headed for the door. "I'll get the box."

Once she was in the bathroom, she told herself not to look in the mirror, but of course she did, and groaned in dismay. Hair going every which way, no makeup, and worst of all, her pink cheeks and sparkling eyes made her look *wholesome*. Tucker had never dated wholesome girls in high school, and she'd bet good money he didn't date wholesome girls now, either.

But then she remembered the way he'd kissed her just now, and there was nothing wholesome about the way she'd kissed him back. She wasn't the shy virgin he'd met outside the school gym that night. She shouldn't be worrying about whether she'd measure up to the other women he'd had.

"Lacey?" he called out from the bedroom. "Is everything okay?"

"Yes," she called back. Grabbing the box of condoms, she walked across the hall and into the bedroom.

Tucker sat up in bed, the covers pulled to his waist. He was leaning casually against a pillow he'd placed between his back and the headboard, but there was nothing casual about the way he looked at her. His gaze was intense, and the hint of a frown creased the spot between his dark eyebrows.

He took a deep breath, and his magnificent chest heaved. "I wondered if you'd changed your mind."

"I haven't changed my mind, but...I'll admit to being a little intimidated by you."

His frown deepened. "Intimidated?"

"You had quite a reputation in high school."

He grimaced. "Don't believe everything you hear."

"Even if I didn't believe all of it, I'm pretty sure that you're more skilled and experienced at this than I am. So..." She paused, her pulse racing out of control. "What if I'm a big disappointment?"

He met her gaze. "I guess it's always possible."

"You think so?" She really hadn't expected him to agree with her. Most men she knew, when presented with a willing woman holding a box of condoms, would brush aside any concerns and get to the action.

"But then, I could be a big disappointment to you, too."

"I seriously doubt that, Tucker."

"After listening to all the gossip, you're probably expecting me to be the best you've ever had."

She couldn't deny it so she said nothing.

"That's a lot of pressure."

She felt ashamed of herself. "You're right. I'm sorry, Tucker. I didn't really think about—"

"On the other hand, it's possible I will be the best you've ever had." His wicked grin flashed. "Why don't you take off those clothes so you can find out?"

She nearly passed out from excitement. She couldn't breathe from the force of it. Now that was the kind of comment she would have expected from him. Heart pounding wildly, she tossed him the box of condoms.

He caught them in one hand without taking his gaze from hers. "For all you know," he said quietly, "I'm expecting you to be the best I've ever had."

Her reply was breathless. "Please don't get your hopes up." With trembling hands, she started removing her clothes.

"Sex is like dancing." Still looking into her eyes, he opened the box of condoms, reached over and upended it on the nightstand. "You're only as good as your partner."

She'd never seen a man empty a box of condoms like that, as if he might need the entire contents eventually and wanted them all available. "That could work both ways," she said. "I could cramp your style." She'd peeled off everything but her bra and panties. If only they were black silk instead of white cotton.

"No, you won't."

She reached behind her back, unfastened her bra and let it slide down her arms to the floor.

He groaned softly. "You *seriously* won't. Look at you."

Her body grew several degrees hotter. "I'm nothing special."

"That's where you're wrong. You're perfect."

No man had ever called her perfect before, and it

must have gone to her head, because as she slipped off her panties, she added a little shimmy to the move.

"You're killing me, Lacey. I need you over here ASAP."

"You do?" She wasn't sure where the temptress voice had come from, either. "Why is that?"

He threw back the covers to reveal his gloriously erect penis. "Does that answer your question?"

She thought she could be forgiven for staring. A girl wasn't treated to something that beautiful every day. In fact, this particular girl had never seen equipment quite so gorgeous.

It summoned an ache from deep inside her, an ache demanding to be assuaged. For the first time in her life she understood the concept of penis envy. If she could have that particular penis available to her on a regular basis, she would be the envy of every woman in the state of Wyoming.

She sashayed slowly over to the bed. She'd never sashayed before, but she was inspired to do it now. "You need to put on its party outfit."

In one smooth movement, he picked up a condom packet from the nightstand and handed it to her. "You can do the honors."

"I'd be delighted." She quivered with eagerness, and even though she'd never been called upon to do this before, she vowed to be cool about it. She ripped open the package. "I've heard moistening it helps."

"You might not like the taste."

"Oh, I bet I will." Heart hammering, she sat on the edge of the bed, wrapped her fingers around his penis and lowered her mouth to the glistening tip.

"I meant the taste of the con—ahhhh...never mind."

She raised her head. "Did I do something wrong?"

"Nope." His eyes had glazed over. "That's great. More of that."

"Okay." Sucking gently, she took him in all the way to the back of her throat and heard him mutter a soft curse. She lifted her head again. "Problem?"

"Uh-huh." His voice sounded strained. "You're very good."

"And that's bad?" He was so velvety soft, yet so deliciously firm that she couldn't resist stroking him.

"It can be." His jaw tightened. "If you keep that up, the party will be over before you know it."

She stopped stroking immediately. "I don't want that."

"Neither do I."

"I thought, with all your experience, you'd be able to—"

"You'd think so, wouldn't you? But watching that curly mop of yours sliding up and down while you... I can't take it."

She touched her hair, suddenly self-conscious. "I know my hair's a mess."

"A wonderful mess." He shoved his fingers into her hair and cradled her head in both hands. "Your hair is perfect for making love all night long." Then he kissed her with such enthusiasm that she forgot all about the state of her hair.

She had to believe that she was perfect, and her hair was perfect, and something about her was so potent that he lost all the sexual control he'd developed over the years. He finally stopped kissing her long enough for her to put the condom on him.

Earlier he must have thought she was going to put the condom in her mouth before rolling it over his penis. She hadn't thought of that, but he'd given her another idea. She was moist in other places, too, and a devilish urge made her put the condom down there to gather up some extra lubrication.

He watched her in rapt fascination. "I'm in serious trouble with you, lady."

"Then let's get into trouble together." She rolled on the condom. By the time she'd finished, he was breathing like a long-distance runner nearing the finish line. "I'm usually a lot calmer about this, Lacey, but…"

"But I get you really, really, hot."

"That's an understatement. Crude as this might sound, you'd better climb on before the train leaves the station."

If she'd been expecting a long, slow seduction where he aroused her to a fever pitch by kissing her all over, she wasn't going to get it, at least not this time. Truthfully, long and slow would have frustrated the hell out of her. She'd gone way past simmer to a full boil, and she wanted him to do her *now*. He could take his sweet time later.

Bracing her hands on his shoulders, she straddled his hips.

"I love your breasts." He cupped them in his large hands. "I haven't paid enough attention to them."

"Don't worry about it." Centering herself over the object of her desire, she wiggled a little to make sure she had him where she wanted him.

He made a strangled sound deep in his throat and his fingers flexed, lightly squeezing her breasts. "Don't wait."

"I won't." And with that, she lowered herself with deliberation, taking him up to the hilt, closing her eyes and moaning as he stretched and filled her. Ecstasy.

He gulped for air and brushed his thumbs over her

taut nipples. Tilting her head back, she reveled in the erotic friction and instinctively responded by starting to lift her hips in preparation for another downward stroke.

Suddenly his hands were there, gripping her tight, holding her down. "Be still for a second. Let me…get my bearings."

She opened her eyes and looked into his. The wild hunger she saw in those green depths made her womb contract.

He gasped. "Lacey…"

"Didn't mean to. I just—"

"I know. Me, too. We might have to go for it."

"I'm in."

His grip tightened on her hips as he held her gaze. "Then ride me, Lacey. Give me all you've got."

Clutching his shoulders and looking into his eyes, she rose up and came down, rose up again and came down faster.

"Yeah." He urged her on, guiding the motion of her hips. "Like that. Like *that.*"

Her orgasm thundered closer with every wild thrust. Her bottom smacked against his thighs, and she began to utter little cries that grew louder, and louder yet. She realized that they were utterly and completely alone. No one could hear, and she could let go as she'd never let go before.

His jaw flexed. "Come for me, Lacey. Come for me!"

She couldn't have stopped her climax if she'd tried. It engulfed her, making her abandon all modesty as she pressed down on that glorious cock and arched into a mindless spiral of sensation. Holding her tight, he drove upward with a bellow of satisfaction, finding the open gate to nirvana and joining her there.

For those few moments, they seemed inseparable. She'd never felt that intensity of emotion, that unique oneness with anyone else. She'd expected polished technique from a man like Tucker. She'd expected pleasure and sinful delight. But she'd never, in her wildest dreams, expected...transcendence.

She wanted to believe she was special, and that the connection had been as unique for him as it had been for her. But that was probably a foolish hope. He was an accomplished lover, the kind of guy who could have almost any woman he wanted.

In a twist of fate, a blizzard had trapped him with her for the night. He'd gallantly made her feel like the only woman in the world for him. He probably did that no matter who he took to bed, and she'd do well to remember that.

5

TUCKER REALIZED SOON after the most profound climax of his life that he was screwed. He'd allowed his hero complex to take over again, and he would pay dearly for that. But hell, she'd been almost engaged to a guy who made *her* buy the condoms.

That had been bad enough, but when he saw the look on her face when she'd thought he was rejecting her hesitant offer to have sex, he hadn't been able to stand it. She deserved so much more than the jerk she'd been going with. Tucker didn't consider himself in the *so much more* category, but he could at least make her feel good on Christmas Eve.

Well, now, he had. From her wild response and the way her body had clenched his during her orgasm, he was certain he'd given her a happy time. And because no good deed went unpunished, he'd just had the most soul-shattering sexual experience of his life.

If history repeated itself, and it usually did, Lacey would either move on or go back to her ex. Either way he was hosed, and this time he wasn't sure how well he'd handle it. True, the rebound guy didn't always get kicked to the curb. He shouldn't automatically assume that Lacey would do that.

He'd love some reassurance that she wouldn't, but how did you ask a woman if she'd felt reality shift in the past few minutes? For all he knew, she always responded with that kind of enthusiasm. He rather doubted it, but trying to find out would be awkward, to say the least. He'd sound like a loser lacking all self-confidence.

She slumped against him, her forehead resting on his shoulder, her breathing slowly returning to normal.

He rubbed her back, marveling at the silky texture of her skin. He'd always imagined that she'd feel like this, but imagining and knowing were such different things. Now he'd never forget the softness under his fingertips. And he'd want to experience it again and again. That might not be in the cards for him.

As he thought about that, he decided on his plan of action. He'd suggested that they celebrate Christmas with a tree, candles, a popcorn garland and a bar of Santa soap. They should follow through on that, and maybe when they weren't in this bed, he'd get an inkling of her true attitude toward him and toward a potential continuation of this relationship.

For years he'd regretted not following up on that kiss. He'd sometimes thought that she couldn't possibly be as perfect for him as he'd imagined. As it turned out, she was even more perfect.

He finger-combed her butterscotch curls. "If we don't get that tree decorated soon, Santa won't leave you any presents."

She stirred and lifted her head to smile lazily at him. "Who needs presents?"

He considered that a promising statement. "Good

point, but after all I went through to bring a tree inside, I think we should put some kind of decorations on it."

She laughed softly. "Nag, nag, nag."

"Did you nuke the popcorn?"

"I did."

"Then let's go string it."

She gazed into his eyes. "You're really serious about this, aren't you?"

"Crazy as it seems, I am. This is the most traction I've ever gotten on the Christmas thing since my mom passed away. I feel a breakthrough coming on."

She nodded. "Then we should honor that."

"Thank you." He was reminded that she was a truly nice person who, if she let him down, would let him down easy.

About twenty minutes later, they'd dressed and laid out their supplies on the kitchen table. She'd volunteered to string popcorn, and he was making a chain of aluminum foil, twisting the foil into links. In his opinion it was an improvement over construction paper and paste, which he didn't have on hand, anyway.

She poked a sewing needle carefully through a piece of popcorn, her head bent and her expression focused. "I'd forgotten how much I like doing this."

He thought about mentioning that she looked adorable stringing popcorn, her rosy lips pursed and her brow puckered in concentration. He decided against saying anything. Too many comments like that and he might scare her off.

Glancing up, she noticed his chain. "That's awesome. I never would have thought of that, but it'll reflect the light."

"We used to cut strips of foil and hang it as icicles, but this is better."

"We need something to give the tree a little color, though." Lost in thought, she continued to string popcorn. Then she glanced up, her eyes alight. "Hershey's Kisses! I just remembered I have a bag of them I brought for snacks. Naturally this time of year they're wrapped in red, green and silver. We can tie threads on them and hang them from the branches!"

"Ingenious." She didn't need Hershey's Kisses when he was prepared to shower her with the real kind. In fact, he already missed touching her, and they'd only been working on this project for ten minutes. At least they'd agreed to only decorate the front of the tree.

A foil chain could be created much faster than a popcorn garland, and soon he had one about twelve feet long. Standing, he draped it on the tree in a zig-zag pattern.

"Very pretty." Her eyes sparkled in that happy way that made his heart swell with satisfaction. "I'm going to remember that trick," she said. "It's really effective."

"Are you saying you might decorate a tree again next year?" God, he wanted to be there if she did.

Her smile dimmed a little. "I don't know."

"I'd help you." He held his breath.

"That would be nice. I mean, if you're available."

"It shouldn't be a problem." He could tell she was hedging her bets, but then, so was he. She hadn't rejected his offer to help her with a tree next year.

He'd take that as a reasonable beginning. "I'll start on the kisses if you want."

She lifted her face to his, her lips curved in a tempting smile. "Which kind?"

Lust slammed into him, but he held himself in check, not wanting her to know just how much he craved her.

Not yet, anyway. Bracing his hands on the table, he leaned in close. "You tell me."

Heat smoldered in her eyes, but then she grinned. "Hershey's, I guess. If you start on the other kind, we'll never finish decorating this tree, and you did haul it in here at great personal sacrifice."

"Now that you mention it, shouldn't you give me at least one kiss in honor of that great personal sacrifice?"

"All right. Just one." She closed her eyes.

He could have moved a few inches and touched his lips to hers, but he didn't.

She opened her eyes again. "I thought you wanted a kiss?"

"I do. I thought you were going to give me one."

"I am. Go ahead."

"Nope. This is my reward, which means you're supposed to kiss *me*."

"Oh. I see the distinction." Putting down her popcorn garland, she reached up with both hands, took him by the ears and pulled him forcefully down to connect with her laughing mouth.

He was laughing, too, but about three seconds into the kiss, the mood shifted. With a soft moan, she let go of his ears, tunneled her fingers through his hair and thrust her tongue in deep. Desperate to feel her against him, he dragged her out of the chair and heard it clatter to the floor.

No matter. Keeping his mouth firmly on hers, he scooped her up, kicked the chair out of the way and carried her into the bedroom. Laying her crossways on the bed, he followed her down as he fumbled with her clothes and she wrenched his shirt open, the snaps popping like gunfire.

He hadn't paid nearly enough attention to her breasts

the first time, but he'd make up for it now. After he yanked her sweater over her head, she arched her back so he could unhook her bra. Soon that joined the sweater on the far side of the bed.

If he'd been hot before, the tactile pleasure of her breasts beneath his hands and mouth turned him into an inferno. He stroked, nipped and tasted until he was wild from wanting her. But he couldn't have her until they'd both rid themselves of their jeans.

Gasping, he pushed himself away from her rosy nipples and stood at the side of the bed so he could shuck his pants. She took her cue from him and wiggled out of hers. That wiggle temporarily mesmerized him as a surge of desire took his breath away.

She wasn't practiced at being seductive, yet somehow she'd turned out to be the sexiest woman he'd ever taken to bed. Every move she made turned him on. He was fascinated by her.

Once she was naked, she scooted around so she was lying lengthwise on the bed. Then she reached for one of the packets on the nightstand, and he realized he was just standing there gaping at her when he should be moving this process along.

Taking the packet from her outstretched hand, he put on the condom. If he only had this glorious opportunity to be with her for one night, he was still one lucky cowboy, and he needed to let her know that.

He could do it by slowing the pace and loving her the way she deserved to be loved, instead of behaving like a rutting bull elk. He moved over her carefully, dropping soft kisses on her cheeks, her eyelids, and finally, on her mouth. "Thank you," he murmured.

Breathing fast, she slid her hands up his chest. "For the condom?"

"That, too." He nuzzled the tender spot behind her ear. "But mostly for allowing me stay with you tonight."

"I couldn't very well let you freeze to death." Her hands roamed around to his back, stroking, kneading, caressing.

"No, but you didn't have to let me do this." He ran his tongue along her collarbone and felt her shiver beneath him. "Or this." Leaning down, he placed a ring of kisses around her nipple.

"Which I hope is leading to this." She grasped his cock and gave it a quick squeeze.

"Lacey!" Lifting his head, he looked into eyes bright with a combination of lust and laughter. "Damn it, I'm trying to be romantic."

She resumed massaging his chest. "I appreciate that, Tucker, but you had the RPMs way up there a few seconds ago, and as a consequence I'm still operating full throttle. How about you drop the clutch and peel out?"

"But I want you to know that I cherish this—"

"I know you do. You nearly froze to death digging up a Christmas tree so I could have a real one to decorate. Then you carried me into the bedroom. No man's ever done that, bodily picked me up and taken me to bed."

"They haven't?" He felt good about that.

"Nope. And let me tell you, it makes a girl feel special to be carried into the bedroom like Scarlett O'Hara."

"Good. I want you to feel special."

"You know what else makes a girl feel special?"

"What?"

"When a guy is so desperate to have her, he can't wait another second. She can see that he has this intense need to thrust deep inside her, to join with her in the most basic way that a man and a woman—"

"Got it." Holding her gaze, he drew back and swiftly buried his cock up to the hilt. The sensation of being inside her while he looked into her eyes made him dizzy with joy. He took a shaky breath. "Like that?"

"Exactly like that." Her blue eyes seemed to mirror the intensity he felt. As she cupped his face in both hands, her words came out in a breathless rush. "If you ask me, this is pretty romantic."

"Glad you think so." He drew back and rocked forward again, moving in tight, locking them together. "How about that?"

"Even more romantic."

"Then, lady, get ready to be romanced out of your mind." He began a steady, insistent rhythm, thrusting deep each time. He felt triumphant as her eyes darkened and her skin flushed pink. Her hands fluttered from his face to his shoulders, and then to his hips. Her fingers dug in as she rose to meet him and began to whimper with need.

As her cries increased in urgency, he bore down, seeking her climax, but also seeking something more, something elusive. He longed to reach the essence of her, to touch that part of her that no other man had ever touched.

Her body moved in perfect time with his as they joined in a race to ecstasy. And then, as if she'd flung open a door, he felt it—her complete and utter surrender. He abandoned the last of his restraint, giving to her as she'd given to him, holding nothing back, driving into her again and again, his cries echoing hers.

Her spasms began a breath before his, and he shouted

with the joy of it as they came and came and came...
together.

For long moments his body shook as he stayed
braced above her. He'd closed his eyes at the very last,
the better to focus on the rolling splendor of climaxing
when she did. But now he opened his eyes and looked
down at her.

She gasped for breath, obviously unable to speak
yet. But her luminous gaze told him more than words
that he hadn't been wrong. Something magical had happened between them.

As her breathing slowed, she reached up and stroked
his cheek. "I love how you make me feel," she murmured.

"That's good." He cleared sudden emotion from his
throat. "Because I love how you make me feel, too." He
had no idea if this magic between them would last for
an hour or a lifetime, but he vowed to be grateful for
the gift and not worry about its duration.

He leaned down and kissed her. "Come on," he murmured. "We need to finish decorating the tree."

"Slave driver."

He lifted his head to smile at her. "You know you
want to."

"I do, actually. I want to see how that popcorn garland looks once it's done."

"See, I knew it. Besides, I think we have a good
system going."

"Oh? What's that?"

"Make love, decorate the tree, make love, decorate
the tree." He punctuated his sentence with more kisses.
"That's working for me."

"Yeah, but eventually we'll have the tree all decorated. Then what?"

He gave her a stricken look. "I guess we'll just have to make love nonstop after that."

"Wow, that sounds drastic."

"I know." He shrugged. "But that's all we'll have left. We'll have to make the best of it."

6

THE SYSTEM WORKED TO perfection, and as Lacey had predicted, they ran out of decorations and ended up back in bed for the rest of the night. Eventually they even went to sleep in that bed, with Lacey nestled inside the curve of Tucker's body.

She woke up in the gray light of dawn with a sense of safety, peace and happiness she hadn't felt in years. Tucker was already up, and the sound of a crackling fire and the scent of evergreen and coffee brewing filled her with memories of waking up as a child on Christmas morning.

Throwing back the covers she shivered in the chilly bedroom as she pulled her blue terry bathrobe and fuzzy blue slippers out of the closet. Of course there would be no presents under the tree, but anticipation bubbled through her anyway. It was Christmas morning and she had someone special to spend it with.

He sat on the couch in front of the fire drinking a mug of coffee, but he put the mug on the end table immediately and stood when she came in the room. His smile flashed. "Merry Christmas."

He'd lit the emergency candles sitting on the mantel,

and light from the fire reflected off the aluminum foil chain and Hershey's Kisses. Her snowy-white popcorn garland was the perfect touch against the dark green branches. As if that weren't enough, a foil-wrapped box lay at the base of the tree. It even had a fluffy white bow.

She glanced at Tucker. "A present?"

"It's not much."

She approached the tree, marveling at how he could have come up with anything at all under the circumstances. No matter what he'd put in that box, she was touched to the point of feeling her throat close up. It was Christmas morning, and a wonderful man had somehow created a present for her to open.

Sitting on the floor beside the tree, exactly as she used to when she was little, she picked up the box, her eyes moist. Then she laughed softly. The ribbon was toilet paper.

She cleared her throat. "You're very clever."

"I used more than I wanted to, because it kept tearing."

"You did all this while I was asleep?"

He nodded and walked over, mug in hand. "It's funny, but I never used to be able to sleep on Christmas Eve. I was always too excited. It's like that feeling sort of came back."

She gazed up at him. "I know what you mean. When I woke up and smelled the tree and heard the fire, it made me all cozy and warm inside, like I used to feel on Christmas morning. Then I walked in here and discovered a present." She patted the floor beside her. "Come and sit with me while I open it."

"Okay, but I hope you're not expecting too much."

He leaned down and set his coffee mug on the floor before sitting cross-legged beside her.

"The fact that this present even exists is a miracle. I didn't think about dreaming up a gift for you."

He shrugged. "Like I said, I was too excited to sleep."

"Well, I'm very impressed that you did this." She tried to get the bow off without tearing it, but it came apart despite her careful effort. "Sorry."

"Hey, it's just toilet paper. Don't worry about it."

"Yes, but you worked so hard to make the bow. I wanted to save it." She tucked the wad of toilet paper in her bathrobe pocket and took off the aluminum foil wrapper. Underneath was a box of graham crackers, except it felt too light to still have crackers in it.

"I put the packets of crackers in the cupboard so I could use the box."

"I am amazed at your ingenuity."

He leaned closer. "Be careful when you open it."

"It's not alive, is it?"

"No, but it's kind of delicate."

She glanced over at him and her heart squeezed. He'd made her something and now he was almost breathless as he waited to find out what she thought of it. Her world shifted in that moment as she fell help-lessly, hopelessly in love.

Opening the top of the cracker box, she reached gently inside and pulled out...a foil angel.

"It's for the top of the tree," he said.

"It's beautiful."

"Hey, are you crying?"

"No." She sniffed and wiped her eyes. "Yes. Oh, Tucker." Laying the angel carefully on the floor next to the tree, she turned to him and climbed into his lap.

He wrapped his arms around her and held her close. "I didn't mean to make you cry."

"They're good tears." She nestled against his warm body and sighed. "Tucker, it feels like Christmas."

"Yes." He stroked her hair. "Yes, it does."

THE MORNING FELT SO RIGHT that Tucker hated to think about leaving. But the storm had ended and he needed to contact the ranch. After attaching the angel to the top of the tree, he shoveled a path to the outbuilding and gave Houdini the rest of the oats and some of the carrots Lacey had left over. Then he texted Jack, who responded that someone would be over with a snowmobile within the next two hours.

Tucker relayed that information to Lacey over breakfast. She'd served him scrambled eggs, bacon and the best cinnamon toast he'd ever eaten. He wanted to stay and spend the day with her, but that wouldn't be happening for several reasons.

First of all, he had to help get Houdini back home. And although Lacey was on vacation, he wasn't. The ranch was short-staffed over the holidays, and he was needed there. He'd made a point of saying he would cover for the hands who'd gone home to their families over Christmas.

He gazed at her sitting across the table from him. She still wore her bathrobe. Without makeup and with her hair still tousled, she looked like a teenager. He thought how wonderful life would be if he could spend every morning across the breakfast table with her.

He put down his coffee mug with a sigh. "I hate to go."

"Couldn't you come back later? Borrow a different snowmobile?"

He shook his head. "Not really. They need me at the ranch." Then he had an idea. "Would you like to come over there for Christmas dinner? I'm sure they'll want to show their appreciation for what you've done, and at least that way we could spend some time together."

She regarded him steadily. "I would love that."

"Great! Dinner's around four. I'll come over with a snowmobile and get you about three, and then bring you back here after dinner. I won't be able to stay all night, but I could stay for...a little while."

"Okay." Her smile told him she knew exactly how they'd spend that *little while.* "That sounds very nice."

It sounded more than nice to him. It sounded promising.

"And by the way, I'm looking forward to seeing all the decorations at the ranch." She swept a hand around the room. "All this has changed my attitude. You were smart to insist on creating our own celebration."

"It worked for me, too. I—" He heard a cell phone, but it wasn't his. "I think you have a call."

"Yeah." She looked disconcerted. "Excuse me." She picked up her phone from the kitchen counter and walked into the bedroom with it.

Tucker wasn't sure how he knew who had called, but he knew, all the same. He'd bet his last dollar Lenny was on the phone. His stomach felt queasy and he stood up, unable to sit any longer. Coffee mug in hand, he paced the living room.

He couldn't hear what Lacey said, but from the low pitch of her voice, he knew the conversation was serious. Maybe something had come up regarding a member of her family. He tried to convince himself this was a family matter, but he didn't believe it. The way things worked in his world, the minute he started getting invested in a woman, something like this happened.

After what seemed like an eternity, she walked out of the bedroom. "That was Lenny."

His stomach pitched. "Oh?"

"He misses me." She looked slightly dazed. "He said he made a terrible mistake by breaking up with me and he wants to get back together. He said he'd find a way to get out here today, so we could spend the holiday the way we'd planned."

He wanted to yell at her that Lenny couldn't come to this cabin and enjoy the tree he'd dug up, or the decorations he'd made, or the woman he'd fallen in love with. Because he was in love with Lacey, probably had been a little bit in love with her for years.

Cruelly, he'd had these few hours to fall completely head-over-heels, and now she would go back to Lenny because that's what women did. They had a great time with Tucker and then went back to their regularly scheduled lives.

He swallowed. "So I guess you won't be coming over to the Last Chance, after all."

"I didn't say that." There was an edge to her voice.

He started the painful process of putting blockades around his heart. "No, but you won't, will you?"

"I don't know, Tucker." She sounded almost angry. "Do you want me to?"

"That's entirely up to you, Lacey." He might have said more, but the roar of a snowmobile cut off their conversation. It was too soon for Lenny to be arriving, so it had to be someone from the Last Chance. Tucker grabbed his hat and coat from the peg by the door. "I need to get going."

"I'm sure you do."

He paused by the door. "Give the ranch a call if you decide you want to come for dinner." He'd deliberately said *the ranch* because he'd never given her his cell phone number and he wasn't going to stop and do it now. He had to get the hell out of there before the pain overwhelmed him. She was going back to Lenny. Goddammit, she was going back to that idiot Lenny!

LACEY STOOD WITHOUT MOVING, her cell phone clutched in her hand. Tucker hadn't been able to get out of there fast enough, and her head was still spinning from his dash to freedom. She could hear him outside laughing and joking with whoever had come to pick him up. It seemed as if he'd already put her out of his mind.

Heartbreaking though it might be, she had to face the possibility that she was simply a bright spot in his life, a person he'd remember fondly but not someone he'd keep around for the long haul. Years ago Tucker had dated lots of girls, but he'd never stuck with one for very long. Maybe he was built that way.

When she'd told him about Lenny, he'd leaped to the conclusion that she was going back to him. Maybe he'd been relieved about that. He'd left the Christmas dinner invitation up to her instead of saying that he really wanted her there. In actuality, she had no idea how much she meant to Tucker. She only knew how much he meant to her.

He'd left before she could tell him what she'd said to Lenny. *What we had wasn't love. I know that, now, because I've truly fallen in love, maybe for the first time in my life.*

How odd that she'd told Lenny, but Tucker was oblivious. If she had any pride at all, he would remain oblivious. Then she looked at the tree in the corner with the angel on top and decided that pride was overrated.

Tucker might not know it, but he had a lot of love to give and she was just the person who could bring it out in him. She wasn't going to abandon her feelings for him because he was too dense to realize he needed her. They needed each other. They'd proved that last night and this morning.

Loving him seemed right, and even if he didn't totally love her back, he had some affection for her. After all, he'd dug up the tree for her, and he'd made an angel to go on top of it. Those two things meant more, in her estimation, than the great sex they'd shared, although that was a bonus. It was good to be turned on by the man you loved.

The sound of the snowmobile starting up prompted her to walk over to the window. They'd tied Houdini's lead rope to the back of the snowmobile and Tucker was just now climbing on behind whoever had driven over to get him. He turned and glanced back at the cabin.

She raised a hand in farewell, even though she didn't think he could see her. But she counted it as a good sign that he'd looked back. He might not be as ready to write her off as he'd seemed. She wondered if pride had kept him from telling her that she meant something to him.

Glancing at the cell phone in her hand, she took note of the time. She'd give him a couple of hours to get situated before she called and asked for a ride to the ranch. She had no intention of waiting until three.

She wasn't nearly through with him, and he wasn't through with her, either, not if she could help it. If nothing else, she could use some help replanting the tree he'd dug up.

TUCKER WAS GETTING DRESSED after a long-overdue shave and shower when the bunkhouse phone rang. He was the only person down there, so he hurried over to the wall phone while he fastened the snaps on his dark green Western shirt. He picked up the phone. "This is Tucker."

"Hey, Tuck." Jack's voice boomed over the phone and raucous noise in the background indicated the Christmas party was starting a little earlier than planned.

Tucker decided from Jack's cheerful tone that he was already into the eggnog. The guy had seemed damned happy to get Houdini back in one piece, and Tucker had now become *Tuck,* which he took as a sign of Jack's goodwill. "What's up?"

"That woman you stayed with last night called here asking if you'd come over and pick her up. She said you invited her for dinner. Did you?"

"Uh…" Tucker's heart lurched into high gear. He'd been so sure he'd never hear from Lacey again, and he had trouble wrapping his mind around this new development. "Yeah, I did. I hope that's okay."

"It's more than okay. Mom's been chewing my ass about why I didn't invite her when I went over there to get you. I wish I'd known you invited her. I could've saved myself some grief. Oh, and tell her to bring an overnight case. Mom won't hear of you taking her back tonight. Too cold."

"She might not go for that."

"Then you'll have to use your manly charm to convince her. Since the fence is still down, you can take the shortcut. I expect to see you both back here ASAP."

"You want me to go now?" Tucker glanced at the bunkhouse clock. "It's only one. I thought dinner wasn't until four."

"That's the official time the food will be on the table, but…hang on." Jack lowered the phone and called out to someone that he had the situation in hand. Then he was back. "Did you hear that? They're bugging me about this lady. What's her name again?"

"Lacey Evans."

"Yeah, Lacey. Gabe and Nick think they remember her from school. Anyway, you need to produce this woman before I end up in some serious shit for lacking good manners. Take one of the snowmobiles. But don't wreck it, okay?"

"I won't. And I'll pay for fixing—"

"Ah, hell, don't worry about it. I just can't afford to lose another one of those machines in the middle of snow season. See you soon, buddy. With the girl," Jack said, ending the call.

Tucker hung up the phone, but he was so distracted that he walked out of the bunkhouse minus his hat and coat. The freezing weather sent him right back in to retrieve them. He'd have to snap out of it or he really would wreck another snowmobile.

Forcing himself to concentrate on one thing at a time, he eventually headed across the snowy meadow in the same direction he'd gone the day before when he'd chased Houdini. He and Jack had retraced this route going back to the ranch, so by now the snowmobile had created a recognizable path in the snow.

That was fortunate for Tucker, who thought far more about Lacey than he thought about driving the snowmobile. He'd worked so hard to banish her from his mind earlier today because he'd been convinced she was reuniting with Lenny. Apparently not. And that meant… He didn't know what that meant, or rather, he was afraid to speculate for fear he'd be slammed again.

No smoke came from the chimney as he approached the cabin, which was a good thing. She couldn't go off and leave a fire burning. But then, she'd know that, being a Forest Service employee.

His chest tightened as he parked the snowmobile near the porch. She'd shoveled most of the snow from the steps and he wished he'd been here to help her. He wished he could walk through that door, close it and stay right here instead of carting her back across the snow to the ranch house where he'd have to share her with a whole lot of people.

As he mounted the steps, the blood rushed in his ears. He hadn't been this nervous about seeing a woman in…he'd never been this nervous, come to think of it.

Lacey opened the door. "Thanks for coming to get me." She stood there looking ready to party in a bright red sweater and crisp jeans. She even had on makeup and gold hoop earrings.

"What happened to Lenny?" He hadn't meant to blurt it out like that, but it was uppermost on his mind and apparently he'd lost control of his tongue. "I thought he was coming out here."

"You thought wrong." She stepped back from the door. "Come in for a minute, Tucker. I have something to say."

He struggled to breathe normally, and when he finally dragged in some air, he got a whiff of the peppermint-soap scent clinging to her. He wanted to gobble her up. He took off his hat, mostly so he'd have something to do with his hands.

She closed the door and turned to him. "Tucker, about Lenny. I—"

"Sarah Chance wants you to bring an overnight bag," he said, deliberately interrupting her. He didn't want to hear about Lenny. Maybe Lenny had been delayed and was coming tomorrow, so Lacey had decided to accept the dinner invitation, after all. "Sarah thinks it's too cold for you to come home tonight, so she's inviting you to stay at the ranch house."

"That sounds great. Now, let me tell you about Lenny."

"I don't want to hear about Lenny, okay? If you've decided to go back to him, that's your business. It has nothing to do with me, so—"

"Tucker, shut up." Walking over to him, she grabbed his face in both hands, pulled his head down and kissed him, hard. The kiss was over in a second and she backed away again. Her eyes glittered as she looked up at him. "Get this straight, cowboy. I don't want Lenny."

"You don't?" An avalanche of relief made him dizzy.

"No. I want you."

He stared at her, not quite willing to trust what he thought he'd just heard.

"I'm taking a chance that you like me enough to give us a shot," she continued. "I realize you're not normally a one-woman man, or at least you didn't used to be when I knew you before, but I'd like you to consider—"

"Yes." He tossed his hat across the room where it landed, he hoped, somewhere in the vicinity of the couch. Then he wrapped both arms around her.

"Yes, what?"

"Yes to being a one-woman man, if you're the woman."

Her beautiful mouth curved in a soft smile. "That's pretty much what I had in mind. I…seem to be falling in love with you."

"Dear God, if this is a dream, I don't want to wake up."

She reached up and pinched his earlobe.

"Ow! What was that for?"

"You're not dreaming."

Still doubting his senses, he gazed down at her. "I must be. The woman I'm falling in love with just said she's falling in love with me."

She went very still. "You're falling in love with me?"

"Yeah." He combed his fingers through her glossy curls. "It's been going on for years, and after the time we've shared in this cabin, it's officially a full-blown case. But I was so sure when Lenny called that you—"

"Why? After our special Christmas, how could you think that I'd go running back to a jerk like Lenny?"

"Because it's happened…a few times before. It seems that I'm generally viewed as a short-term kind of guy."

Her blue gaze grew soft. "Like the girl at the formal, who used you to make her boyfriend jealous?"

"Yeah, or the woman who needed some hot sex to feel better about herself, or the woman who decided that I was fun, but her ex had better career prospects. I could give you more examples, but you get the idea."

"Oh, Tucker." She stroked his cheeks with her thumbs. "No wonder you didn't believe in me. But you will. I promise you will."

He looked into her eyes and saw the love shining there. Only a fool would doubt it. Leaning down, he feathered a gentle kiss over her lips. "I already do believe in you, Lacey." And he kissed her again.

She drew back and placed her finger against his mouth. "Don't we have a party to go to?"

"Good point." Reluctantly he released her, pulled his cell phone out of his coat pocket and hit the speed dial number for the ranch. He wasn't sure who answered because the noise level was so high. "This is Tucker."

He winked at Lacey. "We'll be a little late for the party. Something came up." He disconnected really fast because Lacey had started laughing.

"What?" Dropping the phone back in his coat pocket, he grinned at her as he began unbuttoning his coat.

"You don't think that was too broad a hint?"

"I don't care if it was." He hung his coat on a peg by the door. "It's Christmas and everyone should be allowed to celebrate however they choose." He pulled her close. "Merry Christmas, Lacey."

She smiled up at him. "Merry Christmas, Tucker."

And as he kissed her, he thought about the many Christmas holidays they would celebrate together. They would all be special, because they'd rediscovered the magic of Christmas. But this day, the day they discovered the magic of their love, would always be the most special of all.

* * * * *

NORTHERN FANTASY

Jennifer LaBrecque

An Alaskan Heat *Holiday Novella*

To Vicki and Rhonda, anthology buds extraordinaire.
Happy Holidays!

_1_

JARED MARTIN loosened his tie and collar and ordered a bourbon and ginger ale from the flight attendant, more than ready to trade Manhattan's hustle and bustle for some Alaskan wilderness for a few days. Next to him, Nick Hudson ordered a drink as well.

A light snow fell outside the jet's windows on the first leg of their transcontinental flight from New York's LaGuardia to Good Riddance, Alaska. They'd finish the trip via bush plane from Anchorage to the little town.

"Thanks for traveling across the country during the holidays to be in my wedding," Nick said.

"Anytime." Jared grinned. "Not that I'd recommend you make getting married a reoccurring event." Jared was looking forward to it—the trip, that was. He wasn't big on weddings, especially these days, but he and Nick had been tight since middle school. So when Nick invited Jared to be one of his groomsmen, he'd said yes without hesitation.

"I hear you. I plan to make this a once-in-a-lifetime event, because Gus is a once-in-a-lifetime kind of woman. Damn, I don't know how I got so lucky."

"That's for sure. What she sees in you… Some guys get all the breaks."

Jared had initially thought Nick had lost his mind when he'd turned up for a Saturday afternoon game of hoops eleven months ago and mentioned he was marrying a woman, Augustina "Gus" Tippens, he'd only just met while traveling. That was nuts in Jared's book. And then he'd really thought it was crazy when Gus, a chef, had given up her restaurant in Alaska to move back to New York to work.

However, after actually seeing Gus and Nick together, Jared got it. He was a guy and admittedly not the most "tuned in" or romantic male out there, but even he saw how right and close Gus and Nick were together. They seemed to have a connection Jared and his ex-wife had never had. Jared wondered if he'd ever have something like that.

"Oh, crap. I didn't think before I said that…you know, what with…damn, I'm just stepping in deeper and deeper."

Jared cracked up. Nick didn't fumble often but when he did… "Keep wading, buddy. It's okay. I got a divorce. No biggie."

"Yeah, well, I didn't mean—"

"Nick, it's cool."

The flight attendant dropped off their drinks, one of the benefits of flying first class—first on, first off, and first served.

Nick shook his head. "Trish lost her mind."

Trish. Jared's ex-wife. Funny how quickly he'd learned to think of her that way when for three years he'd thought of her as his wife. Had it really only been nine months ago that she'd announced she was leaving him for her hairdresser? WTF? Who got left for a guy who did hair? Apparently Jared did.

Yep, she'd waltzed in and announced all he ever wanted to do was make money, packed her shit and left. Funny, but Trish had always been more than willing to spend the money he made. He had not, however, bothered to point that out.

True enough he put in a lot of hours, but as a Wall Street trader, staying on top of the game meant staying one step ahead. Trish's leaving had just given him more time to work harder.

He shrugged. "Trish did what she had to do." He'd been surprised at first but then he'd realized the signs had been there—he'd just been too busy to see them. And he'd be damned if he'd ever tell her, but the truth of the matter was he hadn't put much effort—okay, really none—into making their marriage work. He'd taken Trish and their relationship for granted. Now that some time had passed, he could see that.

"Gus has been worried about you."

He and Trish had gone to dinner with Gus and Nick a couple of times. After Trish had bailed…well, Jared had done the only thing he knew, which was immerse himself in work. Gus and Nick had invited him out numerous times after the split but work had just been easier.

"Gus is a sweetheart, but she doesn't need to worry about me," Jared said. He rubbed his hand over his head and tossed out something he'd been considering for a couple of weeks now. "I've been thinking about leaving the city anyway."

"What the hell?" Nick looked genuinely surprised. "You've been thinking about leaving? To go where and do what? You're as New York as they come."

There was a restlessness, a discontent that had been eating at him, that he couldn't seem to shake. "I'm burned out." He'd thought it but it was the first time he'd actually spoken the words aloud to anyone.

"You're serious? Where would you go? What would you do?"

Jared didn't have a clue as to an alternate career and location, he just knew something was missing from his life…and it wasn't his ex-wife. "I don't know yet, I just know I'm ready for a change."

Nick sent him a searching glance, wearing his journalist-on-a-story face. "Are you having a midlife crisis at thirty-one?"

Jared took a healthy swallow of his bourbon and ginger ale. "Possibly." He'd been fast-tracking ever since graduating from Wharton with an MBA and signing on with a prestigious Wall Street firm. He'd met Trish in a martini bar one evening when he was hanging out with some guys from the office after work. A year and a half later, they were tying the knot with a wedding extravaganza followed by a honeymoon in the Seychelles. And the bitch of it was she might say he worked too much, but she wouldn't have given him the time of day if he hadn't been a hotshot Wall Streeter.

And now he was just sick of the whole damned thing. He'd never anticipated being at this place where he was tired of the game. For the first time in his life he no longer knew what he wanted—he simply knew something was missing. "A new career and a new start somewhere sounds better and better. I'd be more than happy to toss in the towel on the condo and the job and try a little dose of being commitment free."

Nick followed another searching gaze with a shrug.

"Then you're heading to the right place. Good Riddance is where you get to leave behind what ails you."

Jared had heard all about Good Riddance from both Gus and Nick. Gus's mother's best friend, Merrilee Danville Weatherspoon, had founded the town twenty-something years ago, when she'd loaded up her RV, left her husband behind in Georgia and drove until she turned up in the spot that felt right. She'd called it Good Riddance. To Jared it sounded as unique and unorthodox, in its own way, as parts of New York.

Jared had read Nick's travel blog with great interest last December, when he'd covered the little Alaskan town's Chrismoose celebration—a week-long holiday festival of arts and crafts, sporting competitions, a Ms. Chrismoose pageant, and a parade. The event was based on a hermit who lived in the wilderness and would ride his pet moose into Good Riddance two days before Christmas.

Jared and Nick were arriving at the tail end of Chrismoose. Traveling any closer to Christmas Eve was too crazy and uncertain, especially when they needed to get to Good Riddance for Nick's wedding.

"It sounds like just where I want to be."

"Well, if you want something different, you damn sure aren't going to be in Kansas anymore, Toto."

It sounded good to him. No New York and no commitments—that just what he wanted in his foreseeable future.

THEODORA "TEDDY" MONROE stood as still as possible while Ellie Lightfoot pinned the bridesmaid dress into place, the fabric a sensual slide against Teddy's skin. Standing still was an unnatural state of being for her.

That is, unless she was playing a role which required her to be dead or sedentary.

Not that those roles came her way very often, which was a direct reflection of living in Good Riddance, Alaska, the middle of nowhere in a state that was about as far as possible from where she longed to be—New York, the place where roles abounded.

One more month and she'd be moving to the Big Apple. Just the thought made it even harder to stand still—she wanted to dance with sheer excitement. She felt as if her whole life was on the verge of blooming wide open—like a caterpillar transformed from the chrysalis stage into a butterfly. This was what she'd wanted for as long as she could remember—to study acting and pursue a career onstage.

Gus and Nick had found Teddy a waitressing gig and a studio apartment in Brooklyn—Manhattan was far too pricey for her budget—right around the corner from Nick's cousin Angela. Gus had sent pictures, warning her the apartment was small. It simply looked marvelous to Teddy, but then again she'd willingly live in a closet as long as that closet was part of the bustle and opportunity of New York.

"Okay, turn around slowly," Ellie said, her dark eyes scanning the fit of the dress. Ellie's glossy black braid, which bespoke her Native heritage, hung over one shoulder. Teddy's dress had been made in New York but shipped to Good Riddance for the final fitting. Ellie was a genius with a needle and thread.

"Don't you just love weddings?" Merrilee said, clapping her hands together. She and Gus sat on the bed. Eartha Kitt's rendition of "Santa Baby," one of Teddy's all-time faves, drifted in through the open bedroom door from the CD player in the next room, adding to the fun atmosphere. Gus had whipped up a gingerbread cake and popped it in the oven. The aroma, maddeningly mouthwatering, permeated the air.

"Any news on your wedding front, Ellie?" Gus asked.

Ellie's quiet smile wreathed her face. "Not yet. We are still waiting on the sign." The entire town had been shocked when Nelson and Ellie had announced their pending marriage and Nelson's plans to pursue medical school. Nelson, who had been training as a shaman, still followed the ways of waiting on answers through signs. Their wedding sign had yet to appear.

Merrilee was obviously delighted by all the wedding trappings strewn about in the bedroom of the apartment above the restaurant Gus used to run. "That crimson velvet is beautiful on you, Teddy. It really brings out your creamy skin and your blond hair."

She'd been a little nervous the color might wash her out, but it worked.

"I do like the rich color." She looked at Gus, the bride-to-be who was also her former employer and friend, who'd flown in from New York two days ago, and smiled. "You did a good job picking out the dresses."

Gus nodded a happy acknowledgment. "I did, didn't I? And they look good on both of Nick's sisters."

Ellie tucked and pinned one more time. "Okay, now let me unzip you and we're done." She tilted her head to one side. "It's beautiful on you."

"Thanks."

It had been a challenge with Gus, Teddy and Merrilee, the matron of honor, in Good Riddance and Nick's sisters in New York. Plus there was an age range from fifty-nine to twenty-four. Teddy had yet to meet Nick's family—they'd be flying in later—but she'd seen pictures. Like him, Nick's sisters had dark hair and startling blue eyes. The dark red would look great on them.

Gus shook her head, looking slightly shell shocked. "I'm not quite sure how it happened but this wedding has escalated to huge."

Teddy stepped out of the dress, taking care to avoid the straight pins, and reached for her jeans.

"It's because you've got a whole new family to embrace you now, honey," Merrilee said with an indulgent smile.

Gus leaving Good Riddance had been hard for Merrilee who loved her like a daughter. But plain and simple, Gus had never belonged in Good Riddance.

Teddy might have been raised in Good Riddance but she no longer belonged here, either. She'd lost her own mother at fourteen, and her father had long before left for parts unknown. But she'd been fortunate enough to have her older sister Marcia, who'd provided a loving, stable home environment.

When she was alive, Teddy's mother had encouraged and nourished Teddy's dream of being a stage actress. After her mother's death, Teddy had found a collection of journals her mother had kept. They'd broken her heart.

Cassandra Monroe had forsaken following her dream of being a classical concert pianist to follow Bill Monroe hither and yon only to have him abandon her and their two daughters in Alaska.

After reading her mother's journals Teddy had grown more determined than ever to make a go of acting, not just for herself but for her mother as well. Teddy had read in the journals that her mother had never wanted Teddy and Marcia to feel as if they were a burden, and it had also just been too painful for Cassandra to talk about the dreams she'd relinquished. So instead of telling her daughters, she'd confined her thoughts to paper and ink.

Working in the restaurant downstairs with Gus for two and a half years, Teddy had set aside every spare penny. Discovering her former fiancé was dead had freed Gus to return to New York.

Lucky, Gus's former short-order cook, had taken over the running of the restaurant in Good Riddance. But it had been critical Teddy stay for at least a couple of months to smooth the transition and to allow Lucky to find and train someone to take Teddy's place, as well. She was helping out during Chrismoose but tonight was her final night at the restaurant.

She'd moved into Gus's apartment above the restaurant to try to get her sister, Marcia, used to the idea of her leaving. Incredibly overprotective of her little sister, Marcia had finally given her blessing on Teddy moving to New York.

She'd begun to wonder if she'd ever leave Good Riddance. Good Riddance was a wonderful place, but it simply wasn't where she'd fulfill her purpose.

Finally, *finally,* everything was in place and in a short period of time she'd be gone.

"I can't wait for everyone to meet Nick's family," Gus said. "You guys are going to love them and they're going to adore everyone here."

Teddy zipped her jeans and tugged her sweater on over her head.

"I'm looking forward to seeing them again," Merrilee said. She and her husband, Bull, had flown to New York in early spring to meet Nick's family.

Ellie carried the dress and they all moved into the open den and kitchen.

"I can't wait to meet them," Teddy said. She was thrilled Nick's family had more than embraced Gus. And once Teddy moved to New York…well, she'd been reassured the Hudsons would take her under their wing, as well.

Merrilee and Ellie settled on the couch while Teddy and Gus moved into the kitchen.

Gus, pulling the gingerbread out of the oven, slanted Teddy an arch glance. "Yeah, well, wait until Nick gets here with his buddy Jared. You'll be glad to meet him, too."

Teddy measured out coffee. She'd kept her love life on hold for several years. Her mother was definitely a cautionary tale. It would've been far too easy to get caught up in a guy and trade in her dreams and aspirations of being an actress for a ring on her finger and settling in Good Riddance, so she'd simply steered clear of any romantic entanglements. "I'm always up for eye candy. And this guy's from New York, so…"

"He's hot. Not as hot as Nick, mind you, but a looker nonetheless." So she'd said earlier when she was giving them the rundown on Nick's best friend. Teddy knew he was a recently divorced stockbroker and a workaholic. She also knew his parents were, according to Nick, pretty awful. He'd categorized them as social climbers who found Jared always just short of the mark. Apparently Jared had spent a lot of time at Nick's house as a teenager. And she knew Nick and Jared met for racquetball once a week.

Teddy added water and turned on the coffeemaker.

She was all for checking him out, but she'd draw the line there.

She wasn't about to be sidetracked by a man at this stage in her life.

2

"WELCOME TO GOOD RIDDANCE, where you can leave behind what troubles you," the venerated Merrilee Danville Weatherspoon greeted Jared when he entered the tiny air terminal that doubled as a bed-and-breakfast and shared space with the town's only restaurant. Clad in a pink-and-gray flannel shirt trimmed in lace, she looked younger than he'd expected.

"I'm happy to be here," Jared said, most sincerely. He'd wanted a change and, by God, this place seemed about as far removed from New York's relentless hustle and bustle as you could get. Even before Nick had pointed it out on the puddle-jumper flight from Anchorage, Jared had already noted the absence of street lights.

However, even in the surreal twilight that enveloped the land, he could clearly see Good Riddance had only one central street and not a single traffic light. One end of town held a plethora of travel trailers, RVs and even a couple of tents for what must truly be the hardy—or rather fool-hardy—souls, all in town for the Chrismoose festival.

Outside it was cold and rather dark, with a fairly

heavy snow falling at four in the afternoon, but inside the "terminal" was reminiscent of some Norman Rockwell wilderness rendering.

A gray-bearded man resided in a rocking chair flanking a chess table next to a pot-bellied stove, apparently engaged in the game by himself. He reminded Jared of some of the old men who hung out in some of the smaller neighborhood parks off the beaten path.

Photos—a haphazard amalgamation of black-and-whites and full-colors, some framed, some not, of people, places and things—covered the timbered walls. Next to the Christmas tree, a full-size plush moose wore a Santa costume. The scents of coffee, hot cocoa, gingerbread and wood smoke hung in the air.

It was a marked contrast to the towering silver tinsel tree outfitted in oversize red ornaments that stood in the lobby of the glass-and-chrome building that housed his office. The homespun charm he found here was a welcome change.

This year he'd elected to forego the tired office winter-holiday party—it was now politically incorrect to refer to it as a Christmas party—where there were actually pools going beforehand as to who would overindulge and make asses of themselves and who would wind up with who in the coat closet, restroom or breakroom. He really didn't care whether he'd looked like he wasn't a team player when he'd passed on the party. He no longer gave a flying flip.

Miracle on 34th Street was playing on the TV in the corner. If there were any miracles to be found on 34th Street he'd missed them thus far. Across the room, a man of Native heritage demonstrated flute-carving to a small but rapt group. Being ensconced in so much hominess *almost* checked Jared's urge to get a final reading on the Dow via his BlackBerry. Good Riddance was just what the doctor ordered. Nonetheless he went online and pulled up the day's final figures. A couple of clicks and he had checked individual stocks. Overall, not a bad closing.

He looked up from his BlackBerry to find Merrilee watching him with raised eyebrows. "Are you back with us now?" she asked.

Going online using a mobile device was *de rigueur* where he came from. Nobody even blinked at it. In fact, it was likely the other person was checking email or texting at the same time as well. However, he suddenly felt as if he'd crossed some line of good manners and tucked his BlackBerry into its case. "Sorry, just needed to check on a few things."

"No problem," Merrilee said. She turned to Nick with a smile. "Gus is holding court next door." *Next door* was the restaurant attached to the terminal and still went by the name of Gus's. "You know how busy it is during Chrismoose, and then word got around Gus was back in town and they're really packing folks in." A door about midway across the room boasted a sign above it, Welcome To Gus's. Even with the television in this room and the small group chatting up front, the muted noise from Gus's was apparent. Merrilee eyed their suitcases. "You probably don't want to work your way through the crowd with that. You can leave them here for now or take the outside entrance."

Gus's living quarters had been above the restaurant. The two-bedroom suite was accessible both from inside the restaurant and from the exterior stairs Nick had pointed out when they landed. Someone else had moved in since Gus left but Gus and Nick were going to share one bedroom and Jared got the couch. Apparently quarters were hard to come by during the Chris-moose festival in Good Riddance. Sleeping on a couch for a few nights wouldn't kill him.

"How about we just leave them here for now?" Nick said.

"No problem." Merrilee waved them to a corner on the other side of her desk. Jared and Nick deposited their luggage before Merrilee hustled them toward the connecting door. "Now get. Go introduce Jared to everyone and I'm sure you're both starving since we're four hours behind New York."

Now that she mentioned it, Jared hadn't really eaten anything all day other than a bagel he'd grabbed on the way to the train this morning. "I could eat a horse," he said.

Merrilee laughed. "You won't find horse but moose and caribou for sure." She shooed them forward. "Bull's bartending. He'll want to meet Jared for sure."

Nick grinned and gave her a quick hug. "We'll see Bull first and then I'll introduce Jared to everyone."

It was good to see the obvious affection between them. Merrilee was as close to a mother-in-law as Nick was going to have. According to Nick, Merrilee had re-sented the hell out of him when he'd first shown up last year. Obviously she'd gotten over it.

A couple came down the stairs to the left of the front door. Upstairs must be the bed portion of the bed-and-breakfast.

As the couple beelined for Merrilee, Nick and Jared crossed the worn wood floor. Nick opened the door to the restaurant, and as the sound had indicated be-forehand, it was mayhem on the other side. Actually, it reminded Jared of a Manhattan happy hour on a Friday evening. To the left of the door the bar area was packed, all the seats taken and several people standing and talking.

Booths lined one wall beyond the bar, and another to the right of the front door, with tables filling in the floor space. To the far right a group was throwing darts, and both pool tables were also seeing action. Jared spotted Gus, with her dark hair—a single swath of signature white in the front—at a large table in the corner.

He nudged Nick. "Gus is over there."

Nick nodded. "Let's meet Bull and grab a drink, then we'll head over."

Working their way to the bar wasn't nearly as quick or easy as he'd thought it'd be. Unlike during a Manhattan happy hour, damn near everyone recognized Nick and stopped him to welcome him back and offer congratulations on the impending wedding. A few of the men jokingly offered condolences. However, everyone they encountered was warm and friendly.

They finally gained the polished bar with the brass foot rail running its length. A stuffed moose head with a Santa hat jauntily angled over one eye reigned amongst the shelved bottles of liquor and glasses on the wall behind the bar. A thickset man sporting a gray ponytail and a full beard was working a draft beer pull. He looked like a Vietnam vet who'd be known as Bull.

He was. Bull and Nick clapped one another on the back and Nick followed up with introductions.

"How was the flight in?" Bull asked.

"Long, but uneventful."

Bull grinned. "Uneventful's always a good thing when you're in the air."

"You bet your sweet ass."

The bar was as busy as the rest of the place. Nick and Jared each snagged a drink and made their way across the room to Gus. After a quick welcoming hug, Gus started the introductions. There were the Sisnukets, a delicate blonde named Tessa and her husband, Clint, reputedly the best Native guide in this area of Alaska. The local doctor, a striking redhead named Skye Shannihan, and her fiancé, Dalton Summers, one of the bush pilots operating out of Good Riddance. According to Nick, the couple was leaving tomorrow to spend Christmas with Skye's family in Atlanta. Nick's crew, his parents, sisters and their families were staying in Summers's two cabins at a place called Shadow Lake. Jared was particularly intrigued when he met a guy named Logan, who had recently moved his corporate job as CFO for a mining operation to Good Riddance so he could marry Jenna, a perky blonde building a spa facility. He hadn't expected to find the CFO of an international enterprise hanging out in this remote town. Jared thought it was cool that with a little help from technology, Logan had managed to pull himself out of the rat race yet still stay in the game.

A Native guy with a long dark ponytail was Clint's cousin Nelson Sisnuket, who worked as a doctor's assistant. The dark-haired woman next to him was his fiancée, Ellie Lightfoot, a school teacher. Across the table, Sven Sorenson could've played the lead in a Viking flick, but was actually a builder.

Jared shook hands with everyone. "Okay, I can't swear I'll remember everyone's name but I'll try."

Across the table, Jenna smiled. "Just blame it on jet lag if you run into one of us and go blank."

Jared was laughing when suddenly the fine hairs on the back of his neck and along his arms stood up.

Gus smiled at someone past his shoulder. "And now you get to meet Teddy."

Jared turned and found himself looking into the prettiest light brown eyes he'd ever seen. Something hot and wild seemed to course through him. He could've sworn the floor literally shifted beneath his feet.

And then he crashed to his knees in front of her.

TEDDY OPENED HER MOUTH but no sound came out. One minute she was face-to-face with a gorgeous guy and the next minute he was on the floor at her feet. She'd never had anything like that happen to her. How did a woman react to that? And well, what did it mean?

The man at her feet had to be Jared Martin. Despite how busy they were, she'd seen him the moment he walked in with Nick. When Gus had deemed him hot... well, that was an understatement. Teddy had written him off earlier as probably too...something. Uh-uh. He was all "just right." Tall and lean with a sculpted face, he looked smart, sophisticated and expensive.

For a moment she would've been hard pressed to even know her own name. It was as if something she'd been waiting on had just walked through the door, but she hadn't been waiting on anything, except the opportunity to get to New York.

Lust was the first thing that had registered in her brain. That he was out of her small-town league had been the immediate chaser thought that followed. And now...what?

Little John, a regular who stood at least six-foot-seven, bent down. "Sorry, dude. I lost my footing and didn't mean to bump into you that way."

Ah, that made sense. He'd been caught off guard and felled by Little John.

Jared regained his feet, brushing at the knees of his

pants. "No harm done," he said to Little John. "A little humiliation is good for the soul now and then."

Good-looking and a sense of humor…and a voice that did all kinds of funny things to her insides.

Little John smiled, nodded and turned back around to his pals. Jared looked at Teddy with a smile that quirked up the right side of his mouth slightly higher than the left. And those eyes…a pale blue that was in marked contrast to his dark lashes. She was, quite uncharacteristically, at a loss for words, her heart thumping like mad against her ribs.

"And now that I've made a stellar impression by literally falling at your feet, it's nice to meet you."

Teddy smiled at his self-deprecating aplomb. She held out her hand, managing to dredge up some semblance of composure. "There's something terribly satisfying in having a man kneel at your feet."

He wrapped his hand around hers. Teddy felt the impact of his touch all the way to her toes. "Does it happen often?" he said.

She was all squirrel-headed from his touch and looked at him blankly. "What?"

"Men falling at your feet?"

He released her hand and she smiled at him. "Absolutely, it happens all the time. I've almost gotten used to it."

"Ah, so I'm just one of many," he said.

With a start, Teddy realized everyone at the table was watching them with avid interest. Gus wore a knowing smirk. For the span of a few seconds Teddy had totally lost track of being in a crowded restaurant. Shaking hands with Jared had been that potent.

Work, Teddy, work, she reminded herself. She needed to focus on work rather than the heat Jared

Martin had unleashed in her. This time she made sure her smile included Nick, as well.

"The specials tonight are caribou stew, moose stroganoff and elk lasagna. What can I get everyone?"

The large group had been having drinks, eating chips and salsa and waiting on Nick and Jared to arrive. It felt so strange to have Gus sitting at the table as a patron rather than being behind the counter running the kitchen. Teddy had missed Gus.

Self-consciousness washed over Teddy. She was altogether too aware of Jared's eyes on her as she took the orders around the table. Of course, she'd had men flirt with her—not only was she a passably attractive female in a state where the men vastly outnumbered the women, she also worked in a bar. She'd selectively dated a few guys, but no one had ever affected her this way. And this man was going to be sleeping on her sofa tonight…and tomorrow night, as well. Of course, she might spend a little time with him and discover he was a jerk. But she didn't think so. She had a feeling her ship was sunk.

3

JARED HAD TO CONFESS he wasn't fully paying attention to the conversation flowing around him. He couldn't seem to stop watching Teddy as she moved about the restaurant. Her energy and enthusiasm captivated him. Her blond hair was up in a ponytail and the way it bobbed and swung as she worked was straight-up sexy. There was nothing overtly enticing about the way she was dressed. She wore jeans tucked into flat, animal-skin boots and a red Christmas sweater with a moose on the front. Jingle bell earrings dangled from her ears. However, there was an inherent sensuality to the way she moved, as if she was extremely comfortable in her own skin. He noticed her in a way he hadn't noticed a woman in a long time, perhaps ever—as if he was seeing nuances and layers he'd never noticed before in other women, his ex-wife included.

More than once their glances had caught and held across the crowded room. As the evening wore on, Jared was increasingly aware he'd buried himself in work for the past nine months with no female companionship since Trish had moved out and they'd divorced.

Next to him, Nick said, "Want to get our luggage

upstairs and settle in a bit, and then if you're still alert and alive we can come back downstairs?"

Jared should've been exhausted given the jet lag and the fact he'd crammed a full day's work into a couple of hours before catching the shuttle to the airport and hooking up with Nick there, but he felt energized in a way he hadn't in a long time. "Sure."

They made their way back through the room, stopping by the bar area to settle their bill. The food had been good, the company great, and watching Teddy Monroe better still. Nick caught her eye and she walked over. "Jared and I are going to take our luggage upstairs. We'll come back down if we're both still alive. Jared's on the sofa, right?"

"Yep. There's a pillow and a couple of blankets." She looked at Jared, the impact of her brown eyes twisting his gut into a knot of hot want. "Make yourself at home. If you find you forgot something you need such as a toothbrush or razor, Merrilee keeps extras next door for the bed-and-breakfast."

"What time do you finish up here?" he asked, getting straight to the point. There'd been any number of interesting conversations going on at the table over dinner, but she was the person in the room he couldn't stop looking at and thinking about.

Teddy's smile left him feeling…he didn't exactly know, but God, she was sexy. "We close at ten and then it's about forty-five minutes to get everything cleaned and ready for the next day."

Nick chimed in. "Don't even bother to offer to help. Trust me, I've seen it firsthand. They have this down to a science."

"Don't let him fool you." Her smile encompassed Nick as well as Jared. "Nick was pretty good at stepping in and taking over when I came down with the flu last year."

Jared remembered the story from when he and Trish had first gone to dinner with Nick and Gus.

Nick shrugged. "We managed. But thank goodness there's no flu outbreak this Chrismoose season."

Teddy nodded. "Yeah, knock on wood." She rapped lightly against the bar's surface for good measure. "I've never been so sick in all of my life. Last year it was a mess with the flu going around."

Jared liked how genuine she was. "That's what I heard."

Lucky called out another order up and Teddy was back in work mode. "Okay, I'll see you guys later."

Jared stood rooted to the spot and watched her walk away, her ponytail swinging and her neat tush swaying.

Nick laughed and elbowed him as they closed the distance to the connecting door between the restaurant and the terminal. "Easy there. You're about one step away from drooling."

Jared shook his head slightly, trying to clear it. They walked into the deserted terminal. A sled dog curled next to the stove raised his head long enough to look at them then lowered it and closed his eyes again. Jared heard someone moving around upstairs.

Leave it to Nick to have summed it up so neatly— Jared wasn't even going to try denying being damn close to drooling over Teddy Monroe. "Hey, she's pretty. Very pretty. What can I say?"

Nick grinned. "It's good to see you back in the land of the living."

"She have a boyfriend?" Not that it would particularly make a difference. Competition was healthy and if she had a boyfriend, Jared would give him a run for his money—he was that damned attracted to Teddy.

"Not as far as I know." Good answer. "In fact, not only does she not have a boyfriend, she's moving to New York next month."

"Are you serious?" Jared grabbed his suitcase. What the hell was wrong with Nick that he hadn't mentioned any of this? Jared immediately felt sheepish. Uh, maybe it was because Nick was getting freaking married.

Nick nodded. "Yep. She wants to go to acting school. She stayed here to help Lucky get on his feet and sock away some extra cash. Gus is going to hook her up with a restaurant job while she's in school. And we found her an apartment just around the corner from my cousin Angela. Remember Angela?" Jared nodded. Of course he did. Angela and her brother Mark had spent nearly as much time at Nick's house as Jared had.

Dammit. Wouldn't you know it? He was ready to check out of the city and a woman who totally blew him away appeared on his horizon? "That's cool. I may not be there by then, but good for her."

"You're really serious about leaving New York?" Nick opened the door leading outside and even though Jared was accustomed to New York winters, the cold hit him like a slap in the face. Snow drifted down in a desultory fashion.

"Yeah, I'm serious." The snow crunched beneath their feet as they walked the length of the building, crossing to a set of stairs on the far rear corner of the building. Small planes sat in the dark on the other side of the small runway to the right.

The muted activity from the restaurant and bar was audible but out here the evening was cold and calm. In the distance a wolf howled. Within seconds the call was answered. Jared looked up. Without the city lights, the sky seemed vast but at the same time close enough that he could touch the velvet darkness.

"This is the other entrance to Gus's…I mean, Teddy's apartment," Nick said.

They climbed the stairs and entered the apartment. Jared stopped in surprise. An open floor plan, sleek furniture, and the odd touch of whimsy here and there reminded him of a Soho loft. This was a definite departure from the frontier décor in the terminal and bar below. A four-foot tree sat on one end table next to the sofa, winking and blinking Christmas cheer from its colored lights.

"Wow, this is definitely not what I expected here." Jared closed the door behind him, shutting out the cold and lightly falling snow.

"That's the same reaction I had the first time I saw it." Nick looked around. "Gus left the big furniture here because it was damn expensive to ship it. She just took photos and artwork. Teddy's brought in her own stuff." The artwork on the wall was all black-and-white prints of theaters and stages and a couple of playbills. Jared itched to pick up and examine more closely a framed photograph on the other end table of three females, one of which looked like a very young version of Teddy. "She's a little more free-spirited than Gus. I love my woman but she can be uptight."

"Gus is good for you," Jared said with a smile but he meant it. Nick's family had always kept him rooted and he needed a woman who did the same. And there was a huge difference in being rooted and being tied down.

"Yeah, she is good for me, isn't she?" Something about Nick's goofy expression touched Jared. He was damn glad his buddy had found Gus. "Well, ace, this is where you're bunking for the next couple of nights. Gus and I are in here," Nick said, walking into a bedroom to the right. "This was Gus's room all along so when Teddy moved in she just took over what had been the guest room." The other bedroom was to the left, with a bathroom in between the two.

Jared sat down on the couch and asked the question he'd wanted to ask since meeting Teddy. "So what's the deal with Teddy? What's her story?"

Nick gave him a quick rundown, bullet-pointing in journalistic fashion. Her father had abandoned the family and then the mother had died. Teddy's older sister had raised her. The sister made a living raising and training sled dogs on the outskirts of town. From what Nick knew from Gus, Teddy hadn't dated much, focusing instead on her family and friends and saving her money for the move.

"So, she not only looks good but she has integrity, too," Jared said.

"And she's a damn nice girl to boot," Nick said on a teasing note. "So, what do you want to do? Shower? Crash? Check out the tube? They have satellite. Or head back downstairs?"

That was a no-brainer. He wanted to check out Teddy Monroe some more. "Definitely head back downstairs."

"OKAY, DONE, AND THANKS so much you guys," Teddy said at ten-twenty. Instead of the customary forty-five-minute cleanup, it'd been done in twenty. Gus, as she had the last several nights, had insisted on helping for old times' sake. Nick had laughed and said he wasn't about to be left out of the party and Jared had good-naturedly claimed he didn't know what he was doing but he could follow directions as well as the next Joe. Not only had it gone fast, but it had been fun.

Teddy admitted it. She was smitten. Jared Martin was the total package. From his sophisticated, but casual good looks, to his sense of humor, to his crisp accent, he was like a Christmas package that had shown up early, wrapped in charm and sexiness. She'd been almost painfully aware of everything about him during their cleanup—where he was, what he was doing, the fit of his shirt over his broad shoulders, the crisp cadence of his voice, the faint whiff of expensive, sophisticated aftershave, and the heat of his gaze. More than once she'd felt him looking at her. It was enough to weaken a woman's knees—well, this woman's anyway.

And while Teddy didn't have a ton of experience, she had enough sense to know when a man was flirting with her and Jared had been flirting all during the cleanup operation.

Gus and Nick stood in the restaurant, holding hands. "If you guys don't mind, we're going to stay down here for a bit. We've got a date," Nick said.

Teddy smiled and sighed inside at how romantic it was. Because there wasn't anywhere to go in Good Riddance on a date in the winter other than Gus's, Nick and Gus had "dated" after hours in the restaurant when Nick had first arrived.

Teddy's heart beat a little faster and harder at the thought of having time alone with this handsome man.

"No problem," Teddy said.

Together she and Jared crossed to the door at the back of the restaurant that opened to the interior stairwell leading to her apartment.

"Don't wait up for us," Gus said with a smile.

"You kids don't do anything we wouldn't do," Nick tacked on, smirking.

On any other given day Teddy might've been embarrassed by Nick's comment but she and Jared had shared one too many heated glances throughout the night. She'd been about five degrees warmer simply with him in the room tonight. And face it, men like Jared Martin didn't come her way every day—well, basically never before.

Teddy closed the door behind them, shutting out the restaurant, plunging them in close-quartered intimacy in the stairwell. Her heart thudded against her ribs and her breath caught in her throat as Jared's arm brushed her waist in the dark, his breath stirring against her hair. The air between them seemed to pulse with awareness.

Teddy flipped on the light switch in the hallway. Laughing at Nick's comment, they climbed the stairs to the apartment.

When they got upstairs, she ushered Jared inside. The lamp was on at one end of the sofa and the Christmas tree lights twinkled in the other end, but other than that the room was cast in shadows.

The air seemed to shift around them and cocoon them the same as it had in the stairwell. "Thanks for pitching in tonight," Teddy said, suddenly at a bit of a loss now that it was just the two of them. She had the totally alien notion she didn't want to sit about making small talk. She wanted to do what she'd longed to do since her first glimpse of him—she wanted to kiss him and be kissed by him.

"It was no problem," Jared said.

It felt different in the apartment with him there. It wasn't as if he was a piece of furniture but it was as if she'd just discovered what had been missing. He should've seemed as out of place as a guy from New York City could seem in an Alaskan village. But, instead, he fit right in with the apartment.

"Are you ready to drop?" she said.

"Actually, I've caught a second wind and I'm wide awake. What do you usually do after you wrap up work? I don't want to interrupt your schedule."

Teddy usually showered when she finished up for the evening but she simply couldn't bring herself to do that now—no way she could strip naked in the bathroom, knowing Jared was one closed door away. The mere notion sent a shiver through her. That felt far too suggestive and intimate and she just couldn't do it, not until Nick and Gus were up here with them.

So, she skipped the showering part and fast-forwarded to the next thing. "I usually have a glass of wine and just sort of decompress," she said, moving toward the dark kitchen. "Would you care for a glass of wine?"

She didn't keep anything stronger in her apartment. She'd noticed he drank bourbon and ginger ale earlier. She'd also noted he'd cut himself off after one pre-dinner drink. She was always aware of stuff like that. Her few memories of her father invariably involved too much alcohol and the unpleasant aftermath. That particular situation had never ended well regardless of what was going on. It had actually been a relief when he'd taken off one day and never came back. How much a man drank and how he handled himself was an issue for Teddy.

Jared stepped into the dark kitchen and seemed to fill it with his presence. "Sure, I'll join you in a glass of wine. And either red or white is fine as long as it's not real sweet."

Teddy laughed breathlessly. "Okay, no Moscato for you."

She poured each of them a glass of shiraz and turned on the iPod docking station. Bing Crosby crooned about a white Christmas. Teddy loved classic Christmas tunes by Bing, Nat King Cole and Perry Como.

"Here you go," she said, handing Jared his glass. Her fingers brushed his and the air seemed to sizzle between them. She settled on one end of the sofa, leaving him the option of the other end or one of the two armchairs. She found it somewhat gratifying he chose the other end of the sofa.

Teddy tucked one leg beneath her, angling in his direction and settled back against the couch's arm.

"So, you're a stockbroker," she said.

"So, you want to be an actress," he said at the same time.

They both laughed.

"You first."

"You first."

"How about ladies first?" he said with a smile that fanned the heat inside her.

That helped to break the ice a little and Teddy found it was easy to talk to him, despite the sexual awareness that seemed to dance through her. She gave him the abbreviated version of her upcoming plans. She was surprised, however, when he knew the school she wanted to attend. It wasn't as if she'd selected the Julliard of acting schools. "You've actually heard of it?"

"I have. It's a great school. My cousin studied there. He's doing some off-Broadway stuff now. When you get to the city I'll introduce you to Gaylord."

"Gaylord?" she parroted without thinking.

Jared grimaced. "I know. Aunt Claudine named him after her favorite grandfather but could she have possibly hung a worse name on him, especially for a theater actor? And by the way, he's not. And there's no good way to shorten his name. He doesn't want to be called Gay and Lord doesn't work either. When he was a kid Aunt Claudine insisted on him going by Gaylord. He goes by Chuck today."

Teddy laughed. "I can see why. And I'd love to meet him this spring." But it wasn't springtime she was thinking about now.

He shrugged, his shoulders appearing all the more broad in his button-down shirt with the Christmas tree lights behind him. For one insane moment, with the tree behind him, it looked as if he were under the tree. And to further her crazy train of thought, Teddy knew without a doubt that Jared Martin was just what she'd like to find under her tree this Christmas. Well, more specifically, she'd prefer to find him in her bed…preferably without all of those troublesome clothes he was currently wearing.

She smiled privately. She'd had the flu last Christmas and it seemed as if she had a fever again now. However, this was a different kind of fever altogether. And she knew precisely what she needed for a cure.

Him.

4

WHAT THE HELL WAS HE thinking? He was alone with a woman he hadn't been able to take his eyes off of all night and he'd brought up his *cousin?* Not only had he mentioned Gaylord, who would have lots in common with Teddy, but then he'd gone out of his way to reassure her Gaylord was straight and offered to introduce them.

"I'm open to meeting as many people as possible," she said, her smile rocking him.

He smiled back. She'd just told him she wasn't caught up in meeting Gaylord because he was a straight guy.

She held her wineglass in one hand and the other arm she stretched along the back of the couch. She rubbed small circles with her finger. Her hands were elegant with short, functional nails. There it was again. It was subtle but she had an energy about her that drew him.

Jared sipped at his wine and copied her, stretching his arm along the back of the sofa, as well. He lightly traced his finger along the back of her hand, leaving her every opportunity to pull her hand away. She didn't.

She simply smiled at him over the rim of her wineglass, her brown eyes taking on a smoky quality.

Her skin was soft and smooth like warm velvet beneath his fingertip. Tension wound between them, beckoned them.

"We just met," he said, leaning in closer.

"I know." Her husky tone stroked through him.

"This is crazy."

"Insane," she agreed. "And I bet you never opt for insanity."

"I never have before."

They both placed their wineglasses on the coffee table and moved toward one another on the couch. Jared leaned in and her breath fanned against his face. There was something almost miraculous about Teddy Monroe, something that got next to him, that tugged at him.

"Would you take your hair down? I've wondered all night what it would feel like."

"You have?"

"I have."

She reached behind her head, her movements sensual and languid, and pulled the elastic out of her hair. With a slow shake of her head, her hair tumbled about her shoulders. She threaded her fingers through it, as if combing it. "Better?"

"Much." He fingered one of the blond swaths. In the lamp light it looked like molten honey and felt like silk. "You have beautiful hair," he said.

"Thank you." She leaned in closer.

He buried his hand in her hair and his fingertips brushed against the back of her neck. She shivered faintly beneath his touch.

And it should feel kind of crazy considering he'd just met her but the strong urge to kiss her simply felt right.

He pulled her to him. Her lips were warm, soft…and potent. Even though she tasted faintly of red wine, the effect was like a shot of smooth, aged whiskey going down. Heat spiraled through him and went straight to his head…both of them.

Teddy deepened the kiss and Jared ran with it. Her mouth opened beneath his and he swept the moist recesses with his tongue. He explored the soft, wet heat of the inside of her cheeks, the velvet length of her tongue. She moaned into his mouth and he swallowed her sound, absorbing it.

Her sweet, hot mouth wasn't enough and he slaked kisses against the line of her jaw, down the column of her neck to the area just below and slightly behind her ear. "Oh, oh, oh," she said, half gasp, half actual words.

Her neck was incredibly sensitive. He teased his tongue against the soft skin and she arched her back and canted her head to one side, allowing him greater access. She grabbed his shoulders and held on to him, her fingers digging into his muscles. Her impassioned response turned him on all the more. Jared felt more alive, more in tune with her than he'd ever felt with anyone before.

He nuzzled at her neck, kissed, and then sucked at the tender spot. It was as if he couldn't get enough of her. He lapped at the delicate shell of her ear, then traced the line with the tip of his tongue.

Meanwhile her touch was warm and arousing as she kneaded the muscles in his shoulders, down to his chest. She found his male nipples through his shirt and teased her fingers against them, the sensation arrowing straight to his penis.

And then they were kissing again. Teddy wrapped her arms around his waist, her hands smoothing along his back. Her kiss was intense, deep, hot. He cupped one of her breasts in his hand and she moaned, pushing harder into his palm. She was just the right size and she felt so good he thought he might explode. Even through the layers of her bra and sweater her nipple thrust against his palm.

His dick was throbbing like nobody's business, straining against the zipper of his pants. He cupped both of her breasts in his hands, massaging and kneading. Her ragged breath matched his.

He'd only just met her, she was a virtual stranger, and he wanted to strip her naked and plunge into her. He wanted to feel the heat of her skin against his own without sweaters or jeans or underwear.

Jared pulled her onto his lap. Linking her arms around his neck, she settled against him.

TEDDY WAS ON FIRE. No man had ever kissed her or touched her like Jared, where she felt as if she were beyond the point of reason. She had never, ever known this frantic need—to have him closer, to feel his hands and mouth against her breasts, to experience the smooth, hot thrust of him inside her. She ached for him. She felt as if every desire she'd ever known was concentrated in her breasts and between her thighs.

Seize the day, the moment, the opportunity urged a part of her she hadn't even known existed. She reached between them and grasped the hem of her sweater in both of her hands. She was on the upward pull when somewhere in the still-functioning part of her brain, she realized something was wrong. Not wrong per se, just different. She heard footsteps climbing the stairs and voices in the stairwell.

Gus. Nick. On their way here. Like a shot she tugged

her sweater back down while scooting back to one end of the couch. She snagged her wine with her right hand and attempted to straighten her hair with her left.

Meanwhile, Jared shifted back to the opposite end and picked up his glass of wine, as well. Teddy glanced pointedly at his crotch where his erection was making itself known by tenting the front of his trousers impressively. He crossed his ankle over his knee which helped. She supposed there wasn't much to be done outside of that.

His voice wasn't quite steady when he said what she guessed was the first thing that popped into his head by way of making conversation other than *I'd really like to sleep with you* which was doubtless his primary thought. "Thanks again for letting me stay here."

"No prob—" Her voice sounded as if it had been dipped in rust. She cleared her throat and tried again, "No problem."

The door opened and Gus and Nick stepped into the room. They both looked startled. "Oh," Nick said, "we thought you'd be in bed by now."

Teddy felt herself blush to the roots of her hair. Hopefully some of it was masked by the room's dim lighting. She hoisted her glass. "We were just getting there. I mean after, you know, we had a glass of wine."

Somehow that didn't make it any better. And she was doubly sure that between Gus's sharp eyes and Nick's nose for ferreting out details and news, they both knew Teddy and Jared had been getting hot and heavy on the couch.

"What he means," Gus said, mercifully, "is he thought Jared would've hit the wall by now."

Teddy stood. "I kept him up talking." He was up all right, but it wasn't because of talking. She didn't dare glance Jared's way. Now that the heat had gone out of the moment, she was moderately mortified.

Jared spoke up, "I got a second wind so I'm wide awake. Teddy was gracious enough to keep me company." He hoisted his glass in her direction. "By the way, the wine is excellent, almost as good as the company."

"Is that a shiraz or a pinot?" Gus asked.

"It's a shiraz," Teddy said, already moving toward the kitchen. "Can I get you a glass?"

"Don't mind if I do," Nick said.

Gus nodded. "Sure, I'll try it."

Her mind whirling, Teddy poured two more glasses of wine. She'd only just met Jared and within no time she'd been on his lap. Another minute and Nick and Gus would've walked in to find her sweaterless. Actually, given the momentum and the heat behind their encounter, she was certain one more minute beyond losing her sweater and she'd have been without her bra as well.

And God knows what Jared must think of her. This was so not her modus operandi. She did not jump on the laps of men like some sex-starved chick—primarily because she wasn't. She wasn't fast and she wasn't easy but she'd just come across as both.

She handed Nick and Gus their wine and retrieved her own. However, she was too jangled to sit down with the three of them right now, which was altogether more disconcerting because she was supposed to be an actress dammit, and she should be able to act her way through this situation, but she simply couldn't.

"If you guys don't need the bathroom right away, I think I'll hop in the shower," Teddy said.

There was a general round of consensus that no one

needed the facilities at the moment so Teddy took her glass of wine and fled to her room.

She was gathering up clean underwear and her pajamas and robe when a knock sounded on her door. She was so jumpy she nearly startled out of her skin. "Yes?"

"It's me," Gus said. Of course it was. Neither Nick nor Jared would knock on her bedroom door. "Can I come in for a second?"

"Sure. It's unlocked."

Gus stepped into the room, her wineglass in hand, and closed the door behind her.

"I told them I wanted to check a wedding detail with you before I forgot it," Gus said. And then in typical Gus fashion, she cut to the chase. "But I really wanted to make sure you were okay."

Teddy took a sip of her wine and nodded. "I'm fine but it was that obvious?" Okay, she was completely mortified. She sank to the mattress's edge.

"No," Gus said, shaking her head. Teddy shot her a disbelieving look. "Okay, it was obvious when we walked in we'd interrupted something but it wasn't a surprise. Jared couldn't keep his eyes off of you all night and you seemed pretty interested, too."

"He's a good-looking man and he's not your run-of-the-mill Alaskan bush male." *That* was a gross understatement. He was urbane and charming and sophisticated…all the things she longed for in a man.

"No, Jared is definitely not that." Gus propped against the door frame. "You look at him and you think East Coast. You look at him and you think The City."

"Right." She looked at him and her entire body broke into a hallelujah chorus of want.

"So, what's the problem? It's only because I've worked with you and I know you so well that I could tell you were upset, but you were definitely upset. What's going on?"

"What's going on is if you and Nick had been a few minutes later, things would've been downright embarrassing. I was about to take off my sweater, and not because he'd asked me to but because I wanted to. I finally meet a man like him and I practically throw myself at him. God knows what he must think of me. You know me, Gus. You know I'm not like that."

"Teddy, I don't believe for a minute Jared thinks anything bad about you. As I said before, he couldn't keep his eyes off of you tonight. When they brought up the luggage, he asked Nick if you had a boyfriend. Nick told him no. And tonight, what would he have seen when he saw you working? You weren't flirting with the customers. You were being you. I can't imagine he thinks you're anything other than what you are—a beautiful, outgoing woman who just met a man she clicks with. And he's a nice guy, Teddy. Trust me, I've seen the way women look at him when we've been out with him. He could've had any woman he wanted after he and Trish split. But as far as I know, and I'd know through Nick, he hasn't dated anyone and I don't think he's slept with anyone."

"Oh." That was good, make it great, to know. He wasn't a player and apparently it wasn't just a case of her being available and willing. If he were so inclined, she imagined he could have women lining up for him back in Manhattan.

"Yeah, *oh*. As far as I can see, you're two nice people who hit a real vein of attraction. Having been there and done that, my suggestion is go for it."

5

TEDDY ROLLED OUT OF bed late the following morning. She had expected to toss and turn all night but oddly enough, after she'd showered and hit the bed, she'd been dead to the world.

Someone was in the shower—she heard the water running. Her bedroom was chilly so she made quick work of dressing. She slipped on jeans and another Christmas sweater, this one green with white snowflakes of varying size outlined in glitter all over it, and fastened snowflake earrings to her lobes. She pulled on thick socks, dragged a brush through her hair and made a quick job of eyeliner and mascara.

She stepped out of her bedroom, the aroma of fresh-brewed coffee greeting her from the kitchen. She usually prepared the coffee pot the night before, but she'd been so disconcerted last night, she'd totally forgotten.

Next to the door, Gus and Nick were putting on their coats. "Morning," they said in unison. Teddy smiled. They really were the perfect couple.

"Good morning," Teddy said. "Where are you two off to so early this morning?" Obviously it was Jared in the shower and obviously he and she were about to be alone again.

"Skye and Dalton left this morning for Atlanta," Gus said, "and we're going to get the cabins ready for the Hudson clan's arrival this afternoon. Skye offered but it hardly seemed fair considering she was working all day yesterday and I've just been doing nothing."

Teddy laughed. "Nothing except getting ready for a wedding." She nodded toward the kitchen. "Thanks for making the coffee."

"No problem. We'll be back in a couple of hours. Jared's planning on checking out the town."

Nick grinned. "At least he doesn't have to worry about getting lost."

Gus punched him in the shoulder and Teddy laughed. "That's for sure. See you guys later."

The door had just closed behind the couple when the water shut off in the bathroom. Teddy moved into the kitchen and poured herself a cup of coffee, but her mind was definitely on the man on the other side of the door—naked and wet. She'd had her hands on him last night, felt the play of muscle beneath her fingertips, and she had no problem picturing him just getting out of the shower.

She turned the radio on in the kitchen, catching the top-of-the-hour local news. Teddy didn't want Jared coming out of the bathroom and to find her just standing around in the kitchen. She needed to be doing something.

While she sipped her coffee, she unloaded the dishwasher. She'd thought when she moved in that she wouldn't really use the appliance since it was just her. Wrong. Every couple of days she had enough to run a load.

She was almost through when the bathroom door opened and Jared emerged. Good grief but he looked good. He wore a pair of jeans with a long-sleeved polo shirt. His dark hair was darker still from being wet. Suddenly, breathing became a challenge.

Teddy aimed for what she hoped was a natural smile. "Good morning. I hope you slept well."

"Fine, thanks. The couch is actually pretty comfortable."

"Good." Okay, they'd exhausted that subject quickly enough. "How about a cup of coffee?"

"Thanks. It smells great." He walked toward the kitchen.

Teddy felt so awkward and it was all her, not him. He seemed fine, normal—well, not that she knew him well enough to gauge normal but he didn't seem uncomfortable at all. The discomfort was all hers and as embarrassing as it would be, she needed to clear the air.

She poured another cup of the fragrant brew and handed it to him. "Sugar's on the counter and there's half-and-half in the fridge. Anything fancier and you're out of luck."

"Straight up is what I prefer." A question glinted in his eyes.

The best thing to do was simply to get this over with. She'd thought that she knew what she wanted to say to him, but now that the time had come, she stumbled through it. "About last night... I don't usually... That's not how I normally—"

Jared shook his head. "Teddy, it's okay. At the risk of sounding as if I'm full of myself, I didn't think last night was your norm. It's not my norm, either, just for the record."

"It's not?" She'd heard it from Gus but she liked hearing it from him also.

He scrubbed his hand through his still-damp hair, leaving it sticking up at a few odd angles. "No. It's not." He reached out and ran his finger lightly down her arm, leaving a trail of heat in his wake.

What was it about him that seemed to reach inside her and touch a part that had never been touched before?

"I'm not sure whether I was relieved or frustrated when Nick and Gus came in," Teddy said, turning away to put the last of the silverware in the drawer.

"Honey, I can assure you I know exactly where I stand on that issue." Jared wrapped one arm around her waist from behind. He pushed aside her hair on the left side and then wrapped his other arm around her, as well. He kissed the side and back of her neck.

She closed her eyes, savoring the feel of his lips against that oh-so-sensitive area. How did he know just the place that did it for her? She wasn't sure if her knees could fully support her as he nuzzled and kissed her neck, taking her from zero to sixty quicker than an Indy car driver.

In his arms, beneath the ministrations of his mouth, her awkwardness vanished, her desire from last night returning in spades. She put her hands on top of his, loving the feel of his masculine, hair-sprinkled skin beneath hers.

She guided his hands up until they were cupping her breasts. "We have unfinished business from last night," she said.

"We do, don't we?" He weighed her breasts in his palms. While his mouth was busy on her neck, he stroked and squeezed. He teased his fingertips against her nipples.

"Why don't we go to your bedroom?" he said. "It might be a little more comfortable than the kitchen, unless you just have a thing for the kitchen."

She laughed softly, turning in his arms. "No, I don't have a thing for the kitchen." Once again, she took his hand in hers and together they made their way to her bedroom. Jared closed the door behind him.

"Nick and Gus will be gone for a couple of hours," Teddy said.

"Good, but just in case…" His smile said he didn't want a repeat of last night. Neither did she.

Outside it was still dark. "Hold that thought." She wasn't sure if she'd ever have this opportunity with someone who turned her on the way Jared did and she wanted to do it right. She darted out of the room and gathered a couple of candles scattered around the den. She also snagged the lighter thingie. She returned, toeing the door closed behind her.

She lit the candles and killed the bedside lamp, casting the room in flickering light.

Jared pulled the edge of his shirt tails free of his jeans and up and over his head. He wore an undershirt beneath. "Layering," he said with a rakish grin. He left on the undershirt, reaching for his belt. Within seconds he'd unbuttoned and unzipped his jeans, as well. He pulled off his socks along with the jeans, leaving him standing before her in an undershirt and briefs.

His arms looked as good as they'd felt last night. There was no mistaking he managed to get in gym time. His quads and calves were muscular. Dark hair sexily sprinkled his forearms and legs. Teddy rather inanely noted he had nicely shaped feet.

She reached for the hem of her sweater and he shook his head, a slow sensual smile curving his lips. "Let me."

She dropped her arms to her sides. Jared grasped the bottom edge, one hand on each side of her, and tugged it up. His hiss of indrawn breath was extremely gratifying when he pulled it up past her bra. Then it was over her head and tossed aside. He moved with surety to the button of her jeans, the backs of his fingers brushing against the skin of her belly as he worked the button free and then slowly tugged down the zipper.

He squatted as he slid the denim over her hips and down her legs. She stepped out of the jeans and he worked her socks down and off as if they were the finest, sexiest silk hosiery rather than thick, practical wool.

"You're beautiful," he said, looking up at her from his position at her feet.

"You don't have to say that."

"I know I don't. I'm saying it because I mean it." He stood and faced her, hesitating. "I was married for three years. After my wife and I split I was tested because she'd been seeing someone else. I haven't been with anyone else. I'm clean."

That was blunt and frank, but Teddy appreciated him bringing the issue up and out. "I...uh...I'm fine, too." It had been over a year since she'd been intimate and she'd gotten a clean bill of health afterward. There was, however, another awkward issue. "I don't have any protection."

"Years ago, my father told me to never leave home without it." His smile held a hard edge. "It was probably the only good advice he ever gave me. I've made it a practice to always carry a spare."

Teddy figured it was a good thing she'd lit candles otherwise the mood might've been totally killed by the practicalities of modern sex.

Jared smoothed his hands over her shoulders. His touch ignited something sweet and hot inside her. Together they lay down on the rumpled, unmade bed. Jared kissed her, a mix of tenderness and eagerness. They were still both in their underwear and Teddy was thankful he seemed to have tuned in to the fact that once they'd trekked to the bedroom, they needed to rekindle the heat they'd found last night in the den and this morning in the kitchen.

It wasn't hard to do. They shared long hot kisses. His hair-roughened thighs pressed against her while he stroked her waist and the curve of her back. The feel of him beneath her fingertips and his scent—fresh and clean, with a hint of tangy aftershave—intoxicated her.

She worked his T-shirt up and over his head, dropping back to the mattress to fully appreciate his physique. He had a nicely muscled, hair-scattered chest. Jared wasn't beefy like some of the guys who worked out too much and he wasn't skinny—Jared's chest was just right, a mix of lean muscle with only a hint of bulk. The trail of hair leading down his belly and disappearing beneath the edge of his briefs added to his sexiness quotient.

"The briefs, too," she said, her voice low and husky, her mouth dry with anticipation while other parts of her were very much wet.

He stood by the side of the bed and did as she'd requested. Teddy didn't have much experience with naked men but what she saw, she liked. His equipment was definitely larger than any she'd seen before but it wasn't grotesquely or even intimidatingly big. Once again, she'd vote for just right.

He knelt on the edge of the bed and slid one bra strap, then the other down her shoulders. He reached beneath her and unhooked her bra. Slowly, as if he were unwrapping a present and wanted to savor the experience rather than ripping into it, he pulled her bra away. His eyes glittered in the candlelight.

He bent his head and languidly licked one nipple and then the other. Teddy felt as if she was coming undone at the stroke of his tongue against her tips. With a groan he took one pink nubbin into his mouth and sucked. Sweet, sweet heaven. He alternated from one breast to the other, leaving her writhing, the area between her thighs drenched, her breasts heavy with need.

Jared kissed his way down her chest and the slight rise of her belly to nuzzle at her panty-covered mound. He licked the inside of one thigh and then the other. Using his teeth, he tugged her panties down past her hips. He hooked his fingers in to finish the material's journey down her legs.

He bent his head, parting her thighs and did what no man had ever done before. He leaned in and kissed her intimately, his mouth and tongue warm and wet and she thought she might just expire on the spot at how good it felt. He kissed, licked and sucked over and over until she was nearly mindless. Finally, when she was clutching the sheets in her fists and thought she couldn't stand it any longer, he raised his head.

"So sweet," he murmured. He slowly slid up her body and kissed her. Teddy tasted herself on his lips. She found it intensely erotic.

He rolled on a condom and spooned behind her.

She'd never had sex in this position but instinctively she raised her top leg to grant him access.

She gasped as he slowly entered her, filling her. He felt good. And then it just got better as he worked in and out. Teddy found her own rhythm, thrusting back against him. He reached around and caught her breast in his hand, squeezing, toying with her nipple.

"Oh, oh, oh," she said in sync with the rhythm they'd both set.

"Here, roll onto your back," he said. At this rate she'd do pretty much anything he requested if it all felt as good as what they'd done so far.

When she was on her back, he positioned himself between her knees and pulled her to him. There was something very arousing about the slide of sheets beneath her, and the strength in his hands and arms. He entered her again and once again she gasped at just how good he felt inside her. Leaning forward on his arms, he was deep into her, her face buried against his neck, even as he buried his face into her neck. His breath was warm and wonderful against her. And then he caught her sensitive skin between his lips and sucked as he ground into her and Teddy's world shattered into a million fragments of light.

6

JARED DIDN'T KNOW WHAT had hit him. He'd never felt like this before. Sex had never been like this, not even with Trish. Not only had it been good, it had been somewhere beyond that. He couldn't even say exactly what it was, but it was out there. And then it struck him—he was content for the first time ever. It had taken him a moment to figure it out, to recognize the feeling, because it was foreign to him. And he'd never really been aware of his discontent before now.

He'd been sated before, sex was good for that. But there was a marked difference in satiation and contentment.

He pulled Teddy closer, her hair against his cheek, her buttocks nestled against his thigh and hip. "How are you?" he asked.

She practically purred. "I'm wonderful," she said, echoing his sentiments. She stretched, shifting against him, and smiled. "I guess we should get up. I'm supposed to be at Jenna's spa—" she glanced at the clock "—in half an hour."

Somehow he found that disappointing. She hadn't struck him as a spa kind of woman—not that there was anything wrong with women who went to the spa, it was just so common in Manhattan. It seemed so many of the women he knew prided themselves on having a high-maintenance reputation. "Got a spa appointment set up?"

She shot him a look that was part amusement and part disbelief. "I've been helping out part-time during Chrismoose when we're swamped with visitors. She was supposed to have her new spa open but a fire delayed that, so now she's working temporarily in part of the community center. She's booked up."

Jared noted Teddy's generosity. She'd signed on to help Lucky transition the restaurant, plus she'd pitched in to help during Chrismoose. And now she was giving Jenna a hand.

"What do you do there? Massage? You certainly have the touch. Not that I've ever had a massage, but if I was going to have one, well, I liked the way your hands felt on me."

She smiled, the smile that seemed to be hers alone, unlike any other. "Hmm, thanks. I like the way yours felt on me as well. But no, I'm not qualified as a massage therapist or any of the other high-brow positions there. I've been covering the reception area and cleaning and setting up the rooms afterward."

Okay, that fit more with the woman he'd just met but already felt as if he knew. She was a mix of earthiness, energy and a slight dreamer quality that showed in her acting aspirations.

Call him uncharitable, but he couldn't help but think that Trish would've been mortified to admit she worked in the capacity of cleaning or setting up anything. Hell, most of the women he knew inflated what they did to make themselves and their jobs sound more important than they were. Hyperbole came with the territory as far as he could tell.

"Do you like working at Jenna's?" he said.

She rolled out of bed, pulling on her underwear. "Sure. I really like Jenna and it's a good way to meet people. Otherwise I'd just be sitting around twiddling my thumbs. As you'll discover, there's not a whole lot to do in Good Riddance."

"How long have you lived here?"

"My family moved here when I was four. I don't remember much at all about where we were before. It's a great place in a lot of ways, but I can't pursue my career here and that's important to me. Everyone has a purpose in life and I think we're all unfulfilled until we discover our purpose and then live it."

It was uncanny how she'd just voiced what had been nagging at him for months now. "And you feel your purpose is acting?"

"No. I *know* my purpose is acting. I've known it from when I was a kid. And now it's time for me to get out there and do what I was meant to do."

He liked her surety and her determination. Far be it from him to ask her if she knew just how damn hard it was to earn a spot on a marquee. He had a feeling she did.

"What about you? You never did say last night. How did you get involved in stockbroking?" She smiled as she tugged on her socks. "It's sort of hard to imagine a kid sitting around thinking they want to run Wall Street."

"Not if you grew up in my house." Success and the world of finance had been part of his life for as long as he could remember. There had seemed to be no viable alternatives. Lately he was thinking it was time for him to review his options. If he left the firm now, he left on a high note, and that was always the best time to go.

"Oh. That doesn't sound like fun."

He grinned. "The fun was always over at Nick's house."

Teddy brushed her hair, static electricity leaving long strands sticking up. She merely grinned at him in the mirror and pulled it back, holding it in place at the nape of her neck with a long barrette. She turned and walked over to the bed and patted his hand. "Don't worry, I grew up in a sucky household, too. But the main thing is we make the best of the hand we're dealt. I'll be finished around one today. Want to meet up at Gus's for lunch afterward?"

"Are you asking me for a date?"

"Well, yes, I am, Mr. Martin."

"Then let's back things up a little because I fully intended to ask you for a date. Want to meet me for lunch today around one downstairs?"

"I'd love to. I'll be the one wearing the snowflake sweater."

"I think I can manage to pick you out of the crowd."

They were joking, but he realized as she closed the door behind her that he could easily pick her out of a crowd, because she was one of a kind.

"You're certainly glowing this morning," Jenna said with a broad smile as Teddy slipped on the black "lab coat" with Spa embroidered in gold across the left breast. Jenna had gone ahead and brought in the accessories for the new place even though it wouldn't be open now until spring.

Teddy did feel as if she was glowing…and floating on a cloud. "Uh-huh."

"I'm thinking this has a lot to do with a certain New Yorker who was at dinner last night."

"It might. It just might." Jared was wonderful. Teddy began folding the clean hand towels in the basket behind the makeshift front counter.

"It's about time," Jenna said, waggling her delicately arched eyebrows.

"I guess it is, isn't it?" She sighed. "It was just so quick."

"That's a shame," Jenna murmured, deliberately misunderstanding her.

Teddy laughed and rolled her eyes. "Not quick that way. I mean, I just met him. I don't really know him."

Jenna waved her hand in dismissal. "That's the way it happens sometimes. Look at me and Logan."

"Uh, you guys went to high school together, Jenna."

Another dismissing brush of her hand in the air pshawed Teddy's logic. "Whatever. I think it's when you least expect it, that it whacks you upside the head."

Teddy paused, but she and Jenna had grown close in the last year. Jenna was a good listener and gave great advice. Teddy could talk to her about things she couldn't talk to her older sister about sometimes. Now would be one of those times. "Jenna, the sex was great. It's never been like that before."

"Double good for you. Make hay while the sun shines. And just think, you'll have someone already in place when you move to New York."

"Well, if we're pulling out clichés, I'm not counting those chickens before they hatch. Good Riddance is one thing, Manhattan is another. I think the competition's a little stiffer there." The very idea made her stomach clench.

Jenna quirked one of her eyebrows. "He's been living

in Manhattan and he hasn't been seeing anyone so apparently that competition's not as heavy-duty as you make it sound."

Teddy wasn't surprised Jenna knew all about Jared. For the most part, there were no secrets in Good Riddance. Except when the occasional secret surfaced it was a doozy, such as when everyone found out that Merrilee hadn't been divorced for the past twenty-five years and was still married to the man they'd thought was her ex-husband. Or when they'd discovered Gus had been engaged to a psychopath who'd stalked her, so she'd changed her name and gone into hiding in Good Riddance. But other than that, everyone seemed inclined to share everyone else's business without compunction, so it was no shock Jenna knew Jared was divorced and hadn't been seeing anyone since his divorce.

"Yeah, well, there's nothing like being in the right spot at the right time. And I believe we can safely assume I'm his post-divorce rebound."

"You never know. It could be more."

"Not on my part and I'm pretty sure Jared's feet are solidly on the ground." Teddy knew that sometimes people thought she was a dreamer because of her acting aspirations. Nothing was further from the truth. Her acting career was a goal. She'd very determinedly saved her money, always with that goal in mind. And most importantly, she'd guarded against getting involved too deeply with anyone, her mother being the proverbial cautionary tale.

No, Teddy would never trade her goals and dreams for a man, any man. She knew firsthand the way that turned out. And the easiest way to do that was to simply have fun but not get too involved. Jared was here for three days. Sex or no sex, emotional involvement wouldn't be a problem. How attached could you get to a person in that time span?

JARED WAS ALREADY SITTING at a table in the restaurant, nursing a cup of coffee, when Nick and Gus came in and spotted him.

"So," Nick said as he and Gus settled at the table. "How'd your morning go?"

Between his activities with Teddy and his subsequent walk through town, Jared couldn't remember a better time. "It's the best day I've had in recent memory. I think I'm in love."

"Say what?" Nick said and Gus did a double-take.

"With Good Riddance. I spent the morning walking around checking out the businesses, meeting people. It's the most laid-back place I've ever been. I really dig it here."

Nick looked at him as if he'd lost his mind. "You realize this is a busy time of year for the town. In fact it's buzzing. There's twice as many people as usual because of the Chrismoose festival."

"Yeah, I get it. It's great! No honking horns, no traffic jams, and you don't have to look past skyscrapers to see the sun. There's fresh snow and trees instead of dirty snow and concrete. The air smells amazing. And there's not a fake Santa on every street corner."

Nick looked at him and shook his head. "You'd go nuts within a month of living here. It's a nice, make that *great,* place to visit, but…"

Given their earlier conversation, he hadn't expected Nick to be so surprised.

Gus spoke up. "Nick's right, Jared. I lived here for four years. It was a haven and the people are wonderful, but it's not New York. I'm fairly certain you'd go stir-crazy."

"Maybe. But then again, maybe not. I think it might take a long time, or it might simply never happen. I like it here."

"Well, good, then we don't have to worry that you won't enjoy the next couple of days."

"Heck, no. You're going to have a hard time getting me on the plane to head back to New York."

Gus laughed. "I'll put Teddy in charge of making sure you make it back to New York. And speaking of the devil…"

Gus trailed off as Teddy arrived at the table. "Speaking of the devil? Me?" Teddy, her eyes sparkling and a smile curving her lips, settled into the empty chair next to Jared. Her arm brushed against his and just that brief touch coursed through him.

"We were just telling Jared we're putting you in charge of getting him back to New York," Gus said. "He's decided Good Riddance is the place to be."

Teddy laughed. "Yeah, right." She looked from Gus to Nick, her laughter dying. "Wait…you're serious?" She looked at Jared as if he'd manifested a third eye. "We have no—" she made a circle with her finger and thumb in case he was missing the point "—traffic lights."

"I noticed."

"Okay, if you say so." Teddy laughed again, shaking her head, but there was a hollow note to her laughter and a hint of a shadow in her eyes. "Are we still on for snowmobiling this afternoon?"

While they took all of this for granted, it was a whole new world to Jared. He'd never been snowmobiling before. He was seriously excited about it. When had his life gotten into such a rut? Hell, maybe he'd been born in a rut and never made a move to get out…before now. Perhaps that had been part of his marital woes. "I'm looking forward to it," he said.

But not as much as he was looking forward to some more alone time with Teddy because all too soon he'd be getting back on a plane for New York, if only to wrap up his affairs there. He was feeling more and more at home in Good Riddance.

7

THE MOMENT TEDDY CLOSED the door, Jared slipped his arms around her from behind.

"I've been waiting all day to do this," he said, nuzzling her neck and pulling her against him.

"Mmm." Teddy offered up a sigh of contentment. "Alone at last."

"My sentiments exactly, but snowmobiling was fun."

"It was, wasn't it? Especially with you behind me."

"You don't know how many times I wanted to kiss you." He teased his lips against the nape of her neck, sending a shiver coursing through her.

She turned, linking her arms around his neck, her internal thermostat hitting a high note. "Gus is taking Nick's mother and sisters to Jenna's spa this afternoon."

"And Nick is taking his brother-in-laws and father ice fishing."

Which translated to alone time in her apartment for them. She teased him. "You didn't want to go ice fishing?"

"I had something else in mind that involved far fewer clothes...."

"Now that sounds like a good idea."

They went into Teddy's room and closed the door. Although Gus and Nick were supposed to be otherwise occupied, erring on the side of caution struck Teddy as a good thing.

"I like your town," Jared said.

"Good. I like your 'town' too."

"That's only because you haven't lived there all your life," he said.

"You might feel differently about Good Riddance if you'd been here since kindergarten, as well." He couldn't seriously be considering staying here. First, he was simply too New York and second, well, it was simply too unfair if he showed up just as she was leaving… And she *was* leaving.

"It's possible."

"Probable," she said. The thought crossed her mind that it was a good thing Jared hadn't turned up in Good Riddance any earlier in her life or she might've been sorely tempted to not leave. But she had a ticket now, and she'd bet after another day or two Good Riddance's rustic charm would wear thin and Jared would be ready to hot-foot it back to Manhattan.

He slid his hands beneath her sweater's hem and caressed her back. His touch, sure and warm, banished all thoughts except how good it felt and how much she wanted more.

They lay down on the bed and took their time undressing one another, exploring, savoring the experience. Everything about this man turned her on—the lean but defined muscles, the smattering of hair on his chest, the texture of his skin against hers, his scent, the way he smiled, one corner of his mouth quirking higher than the other, and the way he moved.

His mouth captured hers and she sighed her satisfaction into their kiss. She cupped his buttocks in her hands—she loved his ass. He had the perfect man-ass—tight, taut and well-shaped.

He was here for such a short time and who knew where things would be when they were both in New York.... She jumped out of bed. "Hold that thought."

She stepped into the walk-in closet and pulled the door closed behind her. She'd played in a production of a farce a couple of years ago in Anchorage. Anchorage was the only "real" theater in the state and that was a stretch. Plus she'd had to fly there and stay with a cast mate for the entire run. She'd played a buxom French maid in the production and she'd had to provide her own costume—nothing like theater on a shoestring budget.

She'd been waiting on this opportunity for a long time. If Jared thought she was weird, he was leaving in two days anyway, so no worries. If he liked it, they'd have a good time. She pulled on black hose with a garter belt, a black lace thong and a frilly white apron, leaving the rest of the costume on a hanger. Slipping on a pair of black heels, she cracked the closet door. Only one thing left. "Close your eyes," she said.

"They're closed."

"No peeking."

"No peeking."

She stepped out of the closet and hurried over to the dresser. She quickly twisted and pinned her hair up and brushed on some red lipstick. She pinned on the frilly little cap that completed the outfit.

She checked herself in the mirror—well, as much as she could see. If Jared wasn't turned on, she was going to look pretty stupid. And if he was...then they'd both reap the benefits.

"You can look now, monsieur," she said with the same accent she'd used in the play. "I am Celeste." The name she'd used before. "I am here to serve you."

"Wow." He propped up on one elbow to get a better look. "Double wow."

This had definitely been a good idea, judging from his reaction and the look in his eyes. She approached the bed. "What would you like, monsieur? I will do whatever you say."

He told her in a low, husky voice exactly what he'd like. Smiling, her heart racing in anticipation and excitement, she climbed up onto the bed and straddled him. His erection pressed against the crotch of her wet panties. "Like this?"

"Oh, yeah." He reached up and traced the edge of her nipple with his fingertip. Oh, yeah was right. He pulled her to him and licked the nipple he'd just outlined. She shuddered and grasped his shoulders. His mouth was warm and wet and just the right combination of gentle and rough as he sucked, licked and nipped her breasts.

"Oh, I like that," she said, careful to keep her voice in character. "That feels so good." Actually it felt better than good. She wasn't even sure what it meant but she threw out whatever came to her in French. *"C'est vrai. Oui, oui, oui."*

Meanwhile, she rubbed her satin-covered mound against the hard line of his penis, her excitement notching higher and higher. She liked having him naked beneath her while she had on the hose and heels and thong and the sheer apron.

He stroked his hands over her hips. Reaching behind her, he grabbed her thong in one hand and pulled gently, tugging it tight between her wet folds. She moaned. *"Oui."*

Teddy's excitement notched up to fever pitch when he told her what he wanted her to do next. Her hand not quite steady, she delved beneath the edge of her panties into her slick channel. Her fingers coated with her essence, she smeared it on his nipple. She repeated it on his other nipple. On instinct, she slowly, deliberately licked each of her fingers before she leaned forward to complete the rest of his request. She dragged her tongue over his eraser-head-hard tips, licking herself off him.

"Oh, baby. That's so, so hot."

She thought so, too.

He rolled on a condom and pulling her thong aside, he guided her up with his hands. Willingly she came down on him, taking all of him inside her at once. She paused for a second, settling on him, rocking against him, and then she rode him so hard and with such enthusiasm that her hair came down and she didn't care. All she cared about was how good it felt, how much they were both enjoying it.

His face tightened and she knew he was close to the edge. He reached between them and found her clit with his finger. Her orgasm exploded inside her and she felt him come right after her. As the last tremors shook her, she collapsed on top of him, incapable of anything more. She felt as if her entire body had become boneless. His breath gusted against her hair. "Thank you," he said.

"Mais, non," she murmured. *"Merci."*

Two days later, Jared stood in his tux behind Nick's best man as Nick and Gus exchanged vows at the Good Riddance community center. Having the ceremony at the community center was a little unorthodox, but it was the only building large enough to hold the crowd that had shown up for the wedding. And altogether Good Riddance was an unorthodox kind of place, so it fit. Gus's restaurant had been a gathering place for the town for several years and Gus was obviously held in high esteem.

Jared's mind wandered as the officiating minister droned on about the sanctity of marriage, his attention snagged by Teddy standing on the bride's side of the lineup. Good God but she was beautiful and sexy in that red velvet dress, her upswept hair leaving her sensitive neck bare. He had no idea how he'd gotten so lucky. Teddy was an incredible woman and not just in the sack, although that was off the charts, too. She was fun, but over the course of the last few days he'd discovered she had a serious side, as well.

Teddy glanced at him, obviously feeling him looking at her. She didn't exactly smile, but her eyes lit up. There was something about her, about them. They were good together in a way he'd never been with anyone else. Yesterday they'd made cookies in her kitchen. He'd never made cookies before in his life—it just wasn't his thing. And quite frankly, if anyone had ever asked him to he would have said thanks but no thanks. But he'd had a great time making gingerbread cookies and decorating them. If he hadn't met her, he would've never known how much fun it could be. What else would he miss out on without Teddy in his life?

Lots. Perhaps everything. As illogical as it seemed, he was far more in love with her than he'd ever been with Trish. She suited him in a way Trish never had. He knew gut-deep that he'd found with her what Nick had with Gus.

He realized with a start that the wedding was over and Nick and Gus were now officially married, when the crowd broke into cheering and the newlyweds took off down the aisle. Within a minute he was holding out his arm to escort Teddy in the best man and matron of honor's wake. It felt very right and natural to have her walking down the aisle on his arm. The idea quickly followed that she belonged by his side.

They followed the other couples back to the dressing area. Teddy sighed. "Wasn't it beautiful?"

Jared wasn't about to disappoint her by admitting he'd zoned out during most of the ceremony. "Yes, it was, and so are you."

It was funny, he'd seen her naked at least twice a day—after that first night, he'd simply moved into her bedroom with no comment from either Gus or Nick—but now a soft blush suffused her neck and face at his compliment. "Thank you."

He ducked into one of the empty rooms, pulling her in with him and closing the door. He backed her up against the door and her arms were immediately around his neck. He kissed her, the need to have her a sudden ravenous hunger inside him. She kissed him back with an intensity that said she felt the same. Once again, that powerful connection flowing between them seemed deeper than mere lust.

"Here. Now. Take me," she said, already pulling up her skirt. One-handed he unzipped his trousers and pulled out his penis which was at full raging attention. While Teddy slid her panties down and stepped out of one leg of them, Jared rolled on a condom. That was good enough. He hooked her leg over his arm and slid into her. Hot, wet and tight she was ever so, so sweet. No other woman had ever felt as good as she did when he was inside her.

They were both excited and further aroused by

making love against a door while the rest of Good Riddance milled about outside. All too soon he felt himself coming. He swallowed her cries as she spasmed around him.

Her breathing was ragged.

"I love you," he said against her forehead. They weren't words he'd intended to say, but nonetheless he didn't regret them.

He didn't know what exactly he expected—well, perhaps a reciprocated sentiment—but he sure as hell didn't expect what he got. Teddy had bent down and pulled her panties back up. Her hand already on the door knob she looked back over her shoulder at him. "We'll just both pretend you didn't say that, and I'm sure it's time we joined the others."

In a flash she had the door open and the opportunity to respond privately was gone.

What the hell? He'd just handed her his heart and she'd tossed it back at his feet. This was not the woman he thought he knew. They might have a reception to get through, but before the day was over he planned to find out just what was going on in her pretty head.

8

TEDDY MOVED THROUGH the reception with a smile on her face but inside her mind was whirling. He'd said he loved her. For one moment her heart had soared in recognition that she felt the same way. And then common sense had kicked in. It was too soon and too dangerous. That falling in love business could wreck her career plans, especially when he was so wrapped up in how great Good Riddance was.

Merrilee came up and put an arm around Teddy. "You sure do look beautiful today. You and Jared certainly make a nice-looking couple."

What was up with everyone today? "Um, thanks," Teddy said.

"Gus is getting ready to throw her bouquet. You need to go get in the group."

"That's okay. I think I'll leave the other ladies to it."

"Nonsense," Merrilee said. "Anyway, it's bad luck for the new bride and groom if all the single women don't join the group. You don't want bad luck for Gus and Nick on your head, do you? Go."

Teddy suspected Merrilee was bending the truth. She'd never heard the part about it being bad luck if all the single women didn't try to catch the bouquet. But then again, there was a lot about weddings she didn't know. For the most part, weddings didn't interest her. While some of the other girls had sat around dreaming of their special day, Teddy had been dreaming of Broadway. Their starring roles had been to stroll down the aisle. Her starring role was to be onstage.

Heels and heart dragging, she joined the group of women ready to vie for the tossed flowers. She stood in the back. Jenna spotted her and cut through the group to tug her up to the front of the small crowd. "Oh, no, Teddy. No hiding in the back."

She didn't have to look to know Jared was watching her from across the room. She felt his eyes on her. "I don't even want to do this," she said to Jenna.

"Sure you do."

The group started a countdown, "Three…two… one…"

Gus tossed the flowers tied in crimson ribbon. It was like a bad dream in slow-mo. Teddy watched as the arrangement headed straight for her like a heat-seeking missile. In the end, she instinctively cradled her arms, unable to allow the bouquet to hit the ground.

Sweet, low-key Ellie stood next to her looking disappointed. Teddy offered her the flowers. "Here. Take them. I don't want them."

"I can't. It's not the same." Ellie smiled, catching Nelson's eye across the room. "I don't need them anyway."

Great! She had a bouquet she didn't want and Ellie had been disappointed. Things were going to hell in a handbasket and it had all started with Jared's declaration. She could kill him for saying he loved her. It had turned everything upside down. She didn't want to talk about or think about love—it complicated everything. Anyway, how could he love her and she'd had some sort of crazy mixed-up feelings for him but how could she love him? They didn't really know one another. People didn't fall in love in three days. That was the stuff of books and movies. And look where it had gotten her mother. Teddy wouldn't be so foolish.

"OBVIOUSLY I SAID THE wrong thing earlier," Jared said. He knew he sounded stiff and awkward but she'd steadfastly ignored him all through the reception until he'd finally corralled her for a dance and she'd have looked bad to have turned him down.

She visibly drew a deep breath. "I just don't know why you said it. We've only known each other for three days."

"It's pretty hard for me to believe, too, but sometimes things happen."

"Yeah and I know firsthand how things can turn out. My mother married in haste and spent the rest of her life repenting at leisure. She gave up her career to follow my dad and he eventually deserted us."

"I'm not asking you to give up anything. I was just telling you how I felt. Have I asked for anything in return except maybe for you to give us a chance?"

"I don't know. I just… My career is important to me. You want to live in Good Riddance and I want to live in New York and that's a fair distance apart."

"I know it is. I would never ask you to give up acting. It's not a mutually exclusive situation. It doesn't have to be me or your career." He could tell by the closed look on her normally expressive face he'd have to pull out everything he had. "Look at Gus and Nick. What was it? Five, maybe seven days? When he first told me

I thought he was insane, but once I saw them together I got it. And look, it's been a year and they're doing great." Damn, wasn't the woman usually the one to do this kind of convincing?

He ran his hand through his hair. He was a man who was used to taking risks. If ever there was a time to put himself on the line, it was now. "I've been doing a lot of thinking. I thought I was burned out at work, and maybe I am, but I can't just walk away from my career and New York. I initially fell in love with Good Riddance, but you're the real draw. You're the sparkle in my life, not the place."

"I have to think. I need a little space."

"Does that mean you want me to sleep on the couch tonight?" It was his last night here. Her answer would be very telling.

"I think that's a good idea."

Damn. That pretty much said it all.

TEDDY TOSSED RESTLESSLY in her bed, unable to sleep. She was doing the right thing wasn't she, staying focused on her career? Now that she was finally prepared to move forward with her dream, she didn't want to make a misstep. But what if she was turning her back on the best man she'd ever met? Was it just some crazy romantic notion that the two of them could have something special in such a short period of time?

She eventually drifted off to sleep. She was dreaming, she had to be, when her mother came to her—the dream was so real she could almost feel the mattress sinking as her mother sat on the bed beside her.

"Mom?"

Her mother didn't say anything but she reached out and smoothed the hair back from Teddy's forehead, a gesture so familiar Teddy's chest tightened with the cherished touch that had been absent from her life for the past nine years. Teddy realized, in her dream, that her mother's smile was different. It was still the same sweet curve of her generous mouth, but the tinge of sadness was gone.

Her mother's lips didn't move but Teddy clearly heard her speak. "Teddy, don't be afraid to love. Your life doesn't have to echo mine if you love. And, darling, my life wasn't a bad one. I had you girls, and I wouldn't trade my time with you and Marcia for any career."

In her dream Teddy could see the surprise on her own face. "You know I read your journals?"

Her mother smiled and continued to speak without actually speaking. "Of course I know, darling. Give him a chance. Give the two of you a chance. Falling in love doesn't mean you can't have a career, too."

Before Teddy could speak again she awoke and her mother vanished as quickly as she'd appeared. Teddy lay in bed, her heart pounding—not from fear but from the exhilaration of seeing her mother, even if it was in a dream. If it had been a dream. Teddy wasn't all too sure her mother hadn't actually appeared before her.

And suddenly the fear she'd felt when Jared told her he loved her disappeared. All her anxiety over her feelings for him dissipated. She realized with a start that things felt so right with Jared she'd been scared, she'd been on standby, waiting for something to go wrong. And it was still a possibility, but she no longer considered it a probability.

Teddy slipped out of bed and padded across the room, opening her door. The couch was empty. Entering the room, she found Jared at the window overlooking town. He had to have heard her but he didn't turn around. She knew she had hurt him. She approached him and slipped her arms around him from behind. Resting her cheek against his back, she said, "I'm sorry."

"Never apologize for being truthful."

"Okay. Then I'll tell you that I…well…I love you, too. I want to give us a chance to see where we go."

He turned, his face cautious, and she didn't blame him a bit given her earlier reaction. "You're sure?"

"I'm positive." She ran her fingers over his jaw. It was amazing how important he'd become to her in such a short period of time. But hadn't she sensed she was a goner from the moment he'd landed on his knees in front of her? "But I don't want you to stay in New York if that's not where you want to be." She'd never do that to another person and their relationship would never survive it.

He caught her hand in his and pressed his lips to her fingers. "Nick asked me on the way out here if I was having an early midlife crisis. All I knew was something was missing in my life. And I know now I've found what I was missing. You."

"Oh, Jared." She wasn't sure whether she wanted to cry or shout for joy, but instead she merely sighed and leaned her head against his chest.

"Teddy…"

"Yeah?"

"You think maybe we could go back to bed now?"

She laughed. Spoken like a true man. Her man.

* * * * *

HE'LL BE HOME
FOR CHRISTMAS

Rhonda Nelson

A Uniformly Hot! Holiday Novella

To Vicki and Jen, my novella mates, for making
this anthology such a joy to write. Merry Christmas!

1

MAJOR SILAS DAVENPORT knew the instant he pulled into the pebbled driveway of his parents' beachside retirement cottage that something wasn't right.

For starters, they weren't there.

No cars in the driveway, no Christmas lights twinkling from the window, no tacky inflatable Santa Claus on the small landscaped yard. Hell, not even a wreath on the front door. His mother was one of those people who typically had her Christmas shopping done by mid-July, so the idea that they were merely out shopping wasn't likely. Dinner then? he wondered. Somehow he didn't think so. There were two newspapers on the front step and the mailbox had been rubber-banded shut, presumably to keep the mail from tumbling out.

His spidey senses started tingling.

He sighed heavily and let himself out of the car, thankful that he recognized the fake rock by the sidewalk that held the hide-a-key. It had been at their old house—the one he'd grown up in—as well.

Well, hell. So much for his surprise, Silas thought, deflated.

He'd just spent the better part of twenty-four hours

in transit. The idea of his family's happy shock when he arrived unexpectedly on their doorstep for Christmas had kept him bolstered. His cheeks puffed as he exhaled mightily.

Instead, he was going to walk into an empty house, no warm greeting or hot meal, no smiling faces, no joyous reunion, no Christmas music playing in the background, no mulled cider warming on the stove.

In retrospect, rather than trying to surprise his family, he probably should have gone ahead and told them that he'd been granted leave. Silas imagined that every soldier in Uncle Sam's Army had applied for leave over the holidays and he'd been no exception. But actually *getting* it was rare, so he hadn't expected he'd have the opportunity to come home. He'd been prepared to spend another miserable Christmas in Iraq, surrounded by men he loved and admired, but who weren't actually his family.

This was the first time in two years he'd been stateside for the holiday and he'd been looking forward to his mother's orange rolls and his dad's homemade wine. To listening to his mother lament his little sister's newest boyfriend—she was currently backpacking across Europe with him, much to their horror—and catching up on all the family gossip. Who was pregnant? Who was engaged? Who was divorcing? The typical grist running through the family gossip mill. It was those little things that made him feel as though he still belonged with his people, was still a member of the tribe, so to speak.

Silas pulled his duffel bag from the backseat of the rental car, then quickly found the key and let himself into the house. It was quiet, as he'd expected, but a pair of women's shoes sat by the front door, as though they'd just been toed off, and he caught the faint sound of music and splashing water.

He frowned, intrigued. "Mom?" he called. "Dad?"

Nothing.

Silas set his bag aside, noting the faint scent of oranges and yeast, and started toward what was actually the key selling point to any beachfront property—the back porch. The house's layout was simple enough. A central set of shotgun rooms—living room, dining room, kitchen—with two master suites on either side of the kitchen, but accessed through short halls off the dining room. Another bedroom, his, was upstairs and had the best view of all. Between the crash of the surf and the scent of his mother's homemade Danishes rising over the kitchen, it was a little piece of heaven—one that he'd been particularly looking forward to.

For whatever reason, he got the grim premonition that he could forget about the orange rolls and usual holiday treats. The fudge, the breakfast casseroles, the ham. The house was chilly, which meant that whenever his parents had left they hadn't anticipated being back for a while and had turned the thermostat down. Secondly, things were too tidy, not lived-in and, though he hadn't seen Cletus—his parents' most recent rescued cat—yet, fresh food was in the bowl.

Were that not enough to clue him in, he'd identified the sound of splashing water coming from the screened-in front porch—the hot tub, specifically—and the music? Ray LaMontagne's "Trouble," accompanied, quite badly, by a woman singing along in a terribly off-key voice.

"Trouble..."

Silas grinned. He'd give her points for being heartfelt, even if he could skewer her performance for technical accuracy.

He carefully opened the back door, spied the clothes on the floor—sweater, jeans, red lacy panties and matching bra—and felt his previously low spirits rise accordingly.

So the mystery woman was naked. In his parents' hot tub.

If she was pretty, too, then maybe his Christmas wasn't going to suck so much after all.

He had a nanosecond to notice curly black hair, a pair of startled cornflower-blue eyes and lush raspberry-red lips...before her mouth opened in a bloodcurdling scream.

DELPHIE MOREAU'S FIRST instinct was to jump out of the hot tub and run for her life, but she was naked and evidently—she'd have to truly think about this later—saving face was more important than saving her life. Clearly something was wrong when a woman would rather *die* than die of embarrassment. She clasped her hands over her bare breasts and wailed for all she was worth.

Seeming startled, the extraordinarily good-looking potential murderer held up his hands in a peaceful gesture and, instead of attacking her, laughed softly. It was a low, intimate chuckle that made her middle go squishy and warm.

"I'm Silas Davenport," he said above her screams. "This is my parents' house."

Ah, Delphie thought, her eyes rounding, the terror dying swiftly in her throat. She paused to look at him and felt a chagrined blush flash across her cheeks. That explained the military garb and the strong resemblance to Charlie Davenport. This man was a taller, much more muscled version of her retired neighbor. Where Charlie's black hair had turned white, his son's was still inky and still very thick. If she hadn't been so startled she was sure that she would have recognized him from the photos in the living room.

So this was the legendary Silas. In the flesh. And what very nice flesh, indeed. Evidently his mother hadn't been exaggerating when she'd extolled the physical virtues of her son. Delphie had imagined that every mother thought her son was handsome and—though he'd certainly looked nice in the pictures she'd seen— occasionally photos could lie.

Clearly the ones she'd seen hadn't.

Furthermore, if everything else his mother had told her was true, then she was half in love with him already.

He grinned at her and wore an expression that brought her sanity into question.

Delphie slunk lower into the water, hoping that the bubbly surface would cover her bare body. She hadn't shaved her legs this morning, she thought dimly. As if it would matter. Sheesh. She was losing her mind. Her face was already flushed from the heat of the water and the two glasses of wine she'd consumed, but impossibly, embarrassment made her cheeks burn even hotter, making her acutely aware of her vulnerable state.

Silas rubbed his hand over the back of his neck. "Er...who are you?" he asked.

Well, yes, he'd want to know that, wouldn't he? Aside from being half-drunk and completely naked, what the hell was wrong with her? She dredged her soul for an ounce of dignity and lifted her chin.

"I'm Delphie Moreau, your parents' neighbor from across the street."

A flash of recognition lit his dark gaze and he inclined his head. "Mom's mentioned you. You're the decorator, right?"

"Interior designer," she clarified. Her skill set was a little more advanced. She didn't just pick out accessories, fabrics and paint swatches. She designed beautiful living spaces based on functionality and a client's needs. She was licensed, knew building code and specs and was handier with a tape measure than a lot of construction workers she knew.

His gaze drifted over her bare shoulders. "Use the hot tub a lot, do you?"

Despite the heat, she felt goose bumps skitter over her skin and her nipples pearl. "Only when I'm keeping an eye on things for them." A thought suddenly struck her foggy mind and she gasped. "You're not home for Christmas, are you?"

Another smile. *Mercy.* "I am, actually."

Oh, no, Delphie thought, wincing. Charlie and Helen were going to be so disappointed. Her gaze slid hesitantly to Silas. Eek! How to tell him?

He waited a beat, then blew out a breath and his eyes widened significantly. "But evidently my parents are not."

She bit her bottom lip and shook her head regretfully. "They left two days ago on a cruise to the Bahamas. With your sister in Europe and you in Iraq they didn't want to face the holiday here alone. They couldn't have possibly known you were coming, otherwise they—"

He shook his head, a silent indicator that she didn't have to finish. "I had the grand idea of surprising them," he admitted with a rueful grimace. "Definitely poor planning on my part. I just never expected them to be gone."

"I'm sorry," she told him. She knew from Helen that Silas hadn't been home for the past couple of years. She couldn't even begin to imagine his disappointment—or theirs, for that matter, when they found out that they'd missed him. They'd be crushed.

"Maybe you could call them," Delphie suggested, grasping at any idea to avoid this outcome. "If there's a way for them to come home, then I know they would."

He pulled a doubtful face. "If they've been gone two days, then they're in open sea," he said. "It would just make them miserable, knowing that I'm here and that they're unable to get to me."

He was right, she knew. Still...

His gaze swept the scene again, lingering on her clothes on the floor, the open wine bottle on the table next to the hot tub and the empty glass. "Sorry for interrupting your party," he said, a smile tugging at his especially sexy mouth. "A special occasion?"

"Not particularly," she said, once again aware of the fact that she was completely naked with a stranger in the room.

Actually, were she to label it, she'd have to say it was a pity party. Her younger stepsister, Lena, was getting married on Christmas Eve. Delphie was happy for her, of course. What kind of person would she be if she weren't? What kind of person begrudges another person happiness?

Unfortunately, while Delphie was genuinely pleased that Lena had found the man of her dreams—when she hadn't even been looking—she couldn't help but feel a little sorry for herself.

Because she *had* been looking. Actively, for over a

year now. She'd found Mr. Maybe, Mr. Wrong, Mr. Right Now, Mr. Asshole and Mr. Possibly-Homosexual-In-Denial, but she'd yet to find her own better half. How unfair was that? Lena was still in college, hadn't figured out exactly what her mark was going to be, much less made it. Hell, she'd met Theo at a drive-thru, for pity's sake. Theo had gotten her French fries and she'd gotten his onion rings. They'd swapped accordingly and fallen in love.

Fried romance.

Delphie, on the other hand, had been out of college for four years, her business was in full swing, quite lucrative and fulfilling. Now she just wanted someone to share her life with. Was that too much to ask?

Thankfully her mother knew that Lena's impending wedding and all the festivities surrounding it were making Delphie even more aware of her own single status and unhappiness, and had limited what she'd asked Delphie to do.

She imagined she'd feel a lot less pathetic if she at least had a date for the wedding, but sadly that wasn't the case, either. Guys tended to get a little squirrelly when a girl invited them to a wedding. You either needed to know someone really well or not at all, otherwise it was a hard sell.

"So are you staying here then?" he asked, derailing her miserable line of thought.

"Er…no. I'm picking up the mail, taking care of the cat and generally keeping an eye on the place." She grinned. "Your parents offered the hot tub and the beach as recompense and I happily accepted." She inwardly frowned.

Of course, now that he was here he could do it.

And she'd lose the flimsy excuse of semi-house-sitting to avoid the wedding festivities.

Not good.

No guy of her own, no date for the wedding and no excuse to stay away from the premarital hoopla.

And she was still naked in front of a perfect stranger.

She knew better than to ask if things could get worse, but couldn't keep from wondering all the same. It seemed to be that kind of day.

And it was that exact moment that she realized she'd forgotten something really important—something critical, even. She felt her face crumple into a wince.

A towel.

2

THOUGH THIS WAS NOT exactly the welcome home he'd imagined, he could do a lot worse than finding a beautiful naked woman in a hot tub, Silas thought. In fact, as far as homecomings went, this was a pretty damned good one.

Delphie Moreau had the most expressive face he'd ever seen.

It intrigued him.

For instance, over the past few seconds he could tell that she'd gone from being mildly worried to unquestionably miserable. Though he wasn't at all certain that he could help her in any way, he was suddenly hit with the irresistible urge to try.

A novelty, to be sure.

Seeing that unhappy expression on such a lovely face made something shift uncomfortably in his chest. Nonplussed, he shrugged the sensation off and tried to remember everything his mother had ever said about her. Honestly, he'd only half-listened when his mom had started in about Delphie. It was quite obvious that she'd had matchmaking on her mind, and Silas had assumed anyone that his mother chose for him wouldn't meet his approval.

He was cursing that wrong-headed conclusion at the moment, though, because given the way his blood had instantly heated and the rapidity with which it was pooling in his groin, Delphie was definitely an exception to that rule.

She was, quite literally, a wet dream.

She had a sweet, heart-shaped face with a sharp little chin, big blue eyes that were large and heavily lashed and a mouth that put him in mind of hot, frantic sex. What little he could see of her petite body was lush and creamy and decidedly feminine. With those shiny black curls piled atop her head and the smooth porcelain of her skin, she reminded him of one of the pretty dolls his mother kept in her curio cabinet.

Her ripe lips formed a hesitant smile. "Could I ask a favor?"

He nodded once, ready to retrieve the moon if she asked for it. "Certainly."

Impossibly, her cheeks pinkened further and she shrunk deeper into the water. Her voice, when she spoke, was small. "Would you mind getting me a towel?"

Silas felt a grin creep over his lips. "No problem."

He backtracked into the house, snagged the requested item out of the linen closet and then returned to the porch and handed it to her. He kept his eyes firmly on her face to keep from trying to sneak a peek at her bare breasts and congratulated himself on his success.

It was a hollow victory.

"Thank you," she murmured. She waited expectantly.

With a belated start, he gestured awkwardly toward

the kitchen. "I'll, uh… I'll just go inside then." Smooth, Silas.

She dimpled gratefully. "I'd appreciate it."

Keenly aware of her every move—he heard the hot tub go off, the tell-tale splash as she left the water—Silas suddenly found himself quite thirsty. He sent a fervent thank-you in his father's direction when he found a lone beer in the refrigerator and made a mental note to buy more.

He'd just popped the top and was in the process of taking a hearty pull when Delphie ducked back into the kitchen. Looking mortified, but more confident, she'd wrapped the towel around what was quite clearly a very petite, very lush frame and held her clothes clutched to her chest. "I'll just go dress in the bathroom."

More torture.

It would have been better if he hadn't seen her undergarments, the red see-through lace, itty bitty scraps of fabric he could imagine shaping her lovely, milky white curves.

Two minutes later—after he'd had time to inspect the contents in the fridge and conclude that while Paula Deen could probably make a gourmet meal out of pickle relish, cream cheese and English muffins, it was beyond the scope of his talent—Delphie returned.

"Well," she said, seemingly at a loss. Her gaze darted around the kitchen, as if reluctant to meet his. "This has been interesting."

He chuckled and passed a hand over his face. "It's certainly added an exciting element to the homecoming story I'm going to tell when I get back," he said. He quirked a brow. "Do you mind if I tell the guys you were wearing a red bow on top of your head?"

Her laugh was quick and throaty, very pleasant. She

pulled a small shrug. "Why stop there? Tell them I had a gift tag around my neck and a no-return policy."

She was quick, too. An admirable quality. "Excellent."

"No batteries required, either." She chuckled and arched a playful brow. "I'm sounding better and better, aren't I?"

"An easy sell, for sure," he said, his gaze skimming over her once again. A particularly sharp bolt of heat nailed his groin. "So you're across the street?"

She nodded. "Yep."

Silas leaned a hip against the counter top, content to study her. She had that kind of face, the sort that drew the eye and didn't want to release it. "How long have you been there?"

"Almost two years."

He inclined his head. "And is there an angry husband or significant other who's going to want to rearrange my face for finding you naked in my parents' hot tub?"

She blushed again, an action he found strangely refreshing. "Er...no."

He brightened. Maybe his Christmas was going to be merry after all, Silas thought, more than a little pleased with the change in his circumstances. Granted his parents weren't in town and this wasn't the homecoming he'd been expecting, but... He pushed off from the counter. "In that case, how about dinner?"

Her startled gaze swung to his. "Dinner?"

"Dinner, supper, the evening meal," he said, listing the various alternatives. "Whatever you want to call it. The fridge is bare and I've spent the last ten hours on a plane eating complimentary peanuts and stale pretzels." He grinned. "I'm hungry. Have you eaten?"

"No," she said. "I find that alcohol is a lot more effective if I drink it on an empty stomach."

That settled it, Silas decided. She was without a doubt the most interesting person he'd met in a long, long time.

Quite possibly ever.

"So you'll join me?" he pressed. He gave her a smile—the one that he pulled out when he really wanted to get his way—and waited expectantly for her answer.

"YES," DELPHIE SAID after a moment's hesitation. Why not? He'd practically seen her naked. What was dinner after that? Furthermore, this was Charlie and Helen's son, a man who'd been serving their country—risking his life—since he'd gotten out of college. How could she say no? What sort of neighbor or patriot would that make her? Delphie wondered, knowing good and damned well that the reason she was saying yes didn't have anything to do with Silas's parents or being a good patriot.

She was a woman and he was *unbelievably* handsome.

He was also a potential wedding date, which had occurred to her while she'd been in the bathroom hastily donning her clothes. Yes, she was being opportunistic, and yes, she should be thinking more about her dear neighbors who were going to miss seeing their son at Christmas. But the shallow, vain part of her couldn't help but think he'd look damned fine on her arm at the wedding. In fact, she wouldn't appear pathetic at all if he went with her.

Glass half full, silver lining and all that.

Silas nodded, seeming pleased with her decision. "Excellent," he said. "Any suggestions?"

"What are you in the mood for?"

"My mother's orange rolls, actually," he confessed with a laughing sigh, "but I don't think I'm going to find those on the menu anywhere in town."

"Ooh, I know of the rolls you speak," Delphie said, following him through the house. "Your mother brought some over to me when I first moved in." He locked the door and pulled it shut. "Do you mind if we stop at my place so I can pick up my purse?" she asked.

"Not at all."

"And you're not opposed to driving? I've only had two glasses of wine, but for some reason it feels like I upended the entire bottle." It was utterly baffling. She hadn't noticed just how unsteady on her feet she was until she'd nearly done a face-plant against the door frame on her way into the house.

He chuckled. "That's because you were in the hot tub. It'll do it every time."

She turned to look at him over her shoulder. "Really?"

He nodded. "Really."

Delphie hummed under her breath and pulled a shrug. "Note to self—always drink in the hot tub. More bang for your buck."

She snagged her bag from beside the door and then walked next to him back to his car. He was even taller than she'd thought, Delphie noted, feeling particularly short beside him. Which, at five-foot-two, wasn't out of the ordinary, really. But for whatever reason, he seemed bigger than other men his height. It wasn't necessarily that there was more of him, but that his very presence seemed to need more room. Interesting.

Thrilling.

Ten minutes later they were snacking on hush puppies, sipping iced tea and waiting on their shrimp and grits. She liked the way his mouth moved when he talked, deep and unhurried, his voice a tantalizing drawl.

"So," he said, staring at her from across the table, his gaze twinkling with intrigued humor. "Do you often drink on an empty stomach?"

Ah. She'd known that little comment was going to come back to bite her on the butt. He waited patiently and seemed genuinely interested in her answer. His close-cropped dark hair had a slight wave and hugged his scalp and his eyes were so brown they created the impression of being black. It was quite arresting. High cheekbones created exaggerated hollows and planes on his face and his nose was appropriately proportioned and straight.

Ultimately, though, it was his mouth that did it for her. A bit full for a man, but masculine all the same, and there was a sensual quality to it that made her feel too itchy in her own skin. It crooked a little higher on one side, an endearing imperfection that somehow made it all the more sexy, all the more charming.

"Drowning a sorrow?" he pressed. "Recent breakup? On the outs with a friend? Someone outbid you on eBay?"

She laughed softly and looked away. "Worse," she said. "My little sister is getting married on Christmas Eve."

His keen eyes sparkled with a little too much understanding. "Ah," he said, lifting his chin. "Feeling left behind then? Like the ugly older sister your father can't unload even with two goats, a dairy cow and a good hunting dog?"

Her eyes widened and she laughed. "Not as bad as all that, thanks," she said. "Just a little melancholy. I'm happy for her," she told him. She squeezed lemon into her tea, then gave it a swirl with her spoon. "But I have to admit I'm not looking forward to the pitying glances from the various aunts and friends, as though I'm a failure compared with Lena's romantic success."

"So it's not that you're envious, you're just competitive?"

"A little of both actually," she admitted, impressed with his intuitive assessment. "But being alone during the holidays is hard enough without throwing a wedding into the mix." She chuckled and pushed a hand through her hair. "It compounds the pathetic factor."

He chuckled and shook his head as though the feminine brain was a mystery. "What is it about women and weddings?" he wondered aloud. "Your sister is signing on as chief launderer, cook, possible incubator and unpaid treasure hunter and you're going all gooey-eyed about it. Listen, it's a bad deal," he said with a deadpan expression, leaning forward as though he were imparting some serious advice. "In a week you're going to feel sorry for her and be patting yourself on the back for your narrow escape."

"Unpaid t-treasure hunter?" Delphie chuckled. Admittedly she got the other references, but this one was lost on her.

"Oh, you know," he said. "Honey, where are my keys? Baby, have you seen my vintage Lynyrd Skynyrd T-shirt?" He shook his head in feigned bafflement. "I've seen brilliant men who can spot bombs beneath a layer of sand get married, and suddenly can't find their asses with both hands anymore. It's amazing, really."

She didn't know when she'd laughed so much, Delphie thought, wiping her eyes. "Well, when you put it like that."

"Trust me," he said, as though confiding an important secret. "I know what I'm talking about. You should feel sorry for her. The romantic little fool has no idea what she's in for."

"I'll keep that in mind," Delphie said, chuckling. *Unpaid treasure hunter.* She mentally snorted, charmed all the same. "But I still wish I had a date."

"I'll go with you," he volunteered, much to her immense and relieved surprise. "We'll fill up on appetizers and make fun of everyone. It'll be fun."

Delphi stilled. Dare she hope? Could she be this lucky? "You don't have other plans?"

Another toe-curling smile. "Er…not anymore, remember?"

"But what about the rest of your family?" Why was she arguing with him? Isn't this what she'd wanted? *Shut up, Delphie.*

"They're still in Arkansas," he said. "My parents retired here, you know." He winced, looking momentarily bleak. "Unfortunately, there is no other family in town."

Her heart drooped for him, and she chastised herself for being selfish. "I'm sorry, Silas. This isn't at all the Christmas you'd imagined, is it?"

"No," he said slowly, releasing a fatalistic sigh. His gaze drifted over her face and settled hotly on her mouth. "But it's improving every minute."

Whoa.

Her nipples suddenly tingled and heat flooded her

belly, then slid south and settled. She pressed her legs together to keep from squirming and mentally calculated the last time she'd had sex. Bleh. Higher math had never been her strength, but she knew from her exaggerated reaction to the man sitting across from her that A plus B in this instance equaled Too Damned Long.

"You'd seriously go to my sister's wedding with me?"

He cocked his head. "Is there going to be alcohol at this wedding?"

"Yes."

"And dancing?"

"Yes to that as well."

"And I'll get to dance with you?" he clarified, pinning her with that hot, dark gaze. "As much as I want?"

Pleasure bloomed in her breathless chest. "If you'd like."

"Sold," he told her with a succinct nod, as if it were a no-brainer.

Relief washed through her, taking away a large portion of the dread. "Thanks, Silas. You're sparing me more humiliation."

"No problem. Besides, I've got an ulterior motive."

A thrill snaked along her spine. She'd just bet he did. "Oh, really? What's that?"

"I'm hoping you'll reward me with a home-cooked meal," he said, surprising her. He popped another bite of hush puppy into his mouth. "It's been too long since I've had one."

She imagined it had. And any chance of his mother's Christmas dinner was down the drain now. No doubt he'd been anticipating that as much as seeing his family. For whatever reason, a meal shared always tasted better.

Or it did to her, anyway. "Anything particular you'd like?"

"Fried chicken, mashed potatoes with gravy and macaroni and cheese," he said without preamble.

"Done," she told him, smiling. "Come over tomorrow evening and I'll hook you up."

Once again that dark gaze drifted across her face and settled on her lips. It was blatantly sexy, ridiculously thrilling and left absolutely no room for misinterpretation.

He wanted her.

Ulterior motive, indeed.

Something passed between them, an unspoken understanding, one that leveled the playing field and made intentions clear. She could have shied away—probably should have considering she'd just met him—and yet... she couldn't. More tellingly, she didn't want to.

Reckless? Potentially stupid? Most definitely. But there it was.

"I'll look forward to it," he said, his voice low and promising.

And from the way her toes were curling, so would she.

3

SILAS HAD NEVER BEEN one to squander an opportunity and, as he walked Delphie back to her door, he had every intention of making the most of this one.

Though the idea of going to a wedding on a date at all—much less a first one—was about as palatable to him as a colonic cleanse, in this case he instinctively knew that he wouldn't regret it.

In the first place, he'd be going with Delphie, the single most intriguing woman he'd ever met. And in the second place, he wasn't going to have enough time at home for this to get awkward. Thirdly, most significantly, she was interested.

He'd watched the flash of awareness kindle in her gaze the moment his eyes had connected with hers and he'd be lying if he tried to claim it was anything other than extremely gratifying.

Admittedly his romantic skills were a bit rusty—all part and parcel of his job—but he still knew enough about women to recognize when one was digging him and, much to his satisfaction, Delphie Moreau was every bit as into him as he was into her.

This brief relationship had the power to be very mutually satisfying and, just to make sure she knew what he was about and to confirm his own suspicions, he fully intended to let her know right now.

She paused at her door and turned to face him. Lamplight glowed golden over her jet-black curls and cast the side of her face in shadow. His breath hitched and a peculiar sensation moved through his chest, one that he'd never experienced before.

"Thanks for dinner," she said. He liked her voice. It was a bit husky, but musical. "I could've paid for mine."

He stepped closer and watched her lips twitch in a smile of recognition. "I asked you out," he said simply. "My treat."

She looked away to hide a smile, then glanced back up at him. Minx. "So that was a date?"

"Definitely. Our first."

She chuckled softly and gave him an admiring glance from beneath her lashes. "You work quick."

He pulled a lazy shrug, not bothering to deny it. What was the point? "I don't have much time."

A little sigh slipped past her lips and a furrow emerged between her sleek brows. "There is that."

"Am I reading this wrong?" Better to ask, he decided.

She considered him for a moment and he watched her gaze flicker to his mouth. "No," she said, seemingly coming to some sort of decision. She looked up at him again. "You're fun."

"Fun? That's all?"

"Fun's good," she insisted, laughing. "Everyone needs to have a little fun."

He was more than willing to give her a lot of it. And here was a small preview.

Silas slipped a finger beneath her chin, gratified

when he felt her shiver, and tilted her face up for a kiss. The first brush of his lips across hers snatched the breath from his lungs and, though he knew it wasn't possible, he felt the ground shake beneath his feet. Startled, he drew back to see if she'd had a similar reaction, and she blinked drunkenly up at him, proof that she found him every bit as intoxicating.

It was all the confirmation he needed.

He bent his head again, this time laying siege against her mouth, and felt her instantly respond. She framed his face with her hands—a gesture that was as enflaming as it was tender—and slid her thumb beneath his jaw. Her sweet tongue moved against his, a mind-numbing seek and retreat that made him instantly hard and unreasonably hot. A low groan sounded in his throat and he wrapped his arms around her, fitting her small body more closely to his. She was lush and ripe and the plum-soft recesses of her mouth made him think of other soft womanly bits, particularly the generous mounds behind her lacy red bra and the even softer skin between her thighs.

He'd either been too long without a woman or this one held some sort of special appeal and, for reasons which escaped him, he didn't want to mine his mind for the answer to that question.

He just wanted her. More fiercely and more desperately than he'd ever wanted another woman.

That thought should have sounded an internal alarm loud enough to rattle his teeth and yet it didn't. He'd have to think more about that later.

Much later. Preferably when it was too late, when he was fitted firmly between her thighs, feeding on her marvelous breasts.

And with any luck, *she'd* be his Christmas present.

SWEET MERCIFUL HEAVEN, Delphie thought as Silas's big hands roamed over on her back and settled hotly on her rear end. She'd been kissed before and had even considered Mr. Wrong a champion kisser…but he didn't have anything on Silas Davenport.

For instance, Silas was one-hundred percent making love to her mouth and yet she could feel it quite keenly in another area farther south. Every time his expert tongue slid inside, her feminine muscles clenched, and with every movement of if his lips against hers, more heat seeped into her decidedly damp panties. Her goose bumps had goose bumps and if her nipples got any harder they were going to shatter. Every bone in her body felt as if it had melted, which was probably why she was practically sliding all over him, Delphie thought.

If she'd ever been so turned on by a mere kiss, then she couldn't recall it. Was it the alcohol? she wondered. Had it really been that much more potent?

No, she decided as he gave her rump a squeeze that made her cling even more tightly to him.

It was him.

He was big and hard and wonderful and when he held her, she felt unbelievably desired and protected, wanted and safe. As a woman who'd always felt more than capable of taking care of herself, it was a bizarre feeling, one that was strangely welcome, incredibly potent.

Aside from being damned good-looking and funny as hell, Silas Davenport had that other something special, that indefinable quality that gave him an edge over every other guy.

And she was cooking dinner for him tomorrow night *and* he was going to the wedding with her. The only thing that could make this day better was an orgasm, and she was dangerously close to getting that, too.

But not on the first date.

Breathing heavily, she reluctantly ended the kiss.

"Wow," he said, the admiration in his tone making her blush with pleasure. "I'd take you without the hunting dog," he teased.

Delphie chuckled. "Thanks," she said drolly. "I'll be sure to pass that along to my father."

He grinned down at her, his dark eyes twinkling with humor. "What time do you want me?"

She blinked up at him, momentarily panicked. She actually wanted him right now, but didn't think she was in the best condition to be making that decision. Was it inevitable? Oh, yes. She'd known that over dinner. But tonight?

His head dropped back and he laughed. "I mean for dinner," he told her.

Ah. Of course. She squeezed her eyes tightly shut as more color burst upon her cheeks. "Five work for you?"

"I'm available all day," he said, shooting a forlorn look across the street to the empty house.

A blatant ploy. "I'm sure you'll find something to do," she drawled.

From the look on his face, he thought he already had—*her*.

And the kicker? He was right.

In that instant she knew beyond a shadow of a doubt that at some point before he left for Iraq again they were going to fall into bed together.

She wanted. She ached. She yearned.

And for reasons which escaped her, she felt bizarrely *secure* with him, for lack of a better description. It was as though a part of her that was always wound tight and on guard could relax with him, simply let go, and that feeling was so inexplicably wonderful she didn't know what to make of it.

Furthermore, the way her libido was humming, they'd be damned lucky if they made it to a bed. In fact, if this had been their third date—her usual absolute minimum before intimacy—he more than likely could have taken her right here on her front porch.

The thought was as disconcerting as it was thrilling, and should have set off an alarm strong enough to wake the dead.

Delphie merely smiled.

She was too excited to be spooked and too turned on to be cautious. Sometimes the best plan was no plan at all.

4

AT FIVE O'CLOCK ON THE dot, Silas rang Delphie's door bell. He'd been bored out of his skull *all day*. He'd taken care of some things around the house for his parents—a lightbulb had blown out in the carport and he'd fixed a loose step on the back porch—and had made a trip to the grocery store. He still needed to pick up a few Christmas presents for his parents and his sister, but had decided to pace himself, lest he run out of anything to do and embarrass himself by trying to hang out with Delphie all day.

Though he wouldn't have ever considered himself the sentimental Christmas type, Silas had discovered that he was missing more about the holiday than just his parents. He'd broodingly considered the absence of the Christmas tree and decorations and, after a few minutes of debate where he questioned his sanity, he dragged the decorations out of the attic and started putting them around the house.

The tree, the Nativity, the candle-holding Mrs. Claus who played "Jingle Bells," the battered wreath for the front door. He'd found the Christmas CDs and had plugged them into the DVD player and, in absence of the knowledge of how to make mulled cider, had lit a cinnamon candle he'd found in the kitchen. Once finished, he'd proudly inspected his handiwork and most definitely felt more of the holiday spirit taking hold.

Because he'd seen another person walking their cat on a leash down the beach, he'd picked one up and given it a try with Cletus.

To his delight, it had worked.

Initially the cat had looked at him as if he'd lost his mind, but after a few false starts Cletus had decided that he enjoyed being outside, even if he was tethered to a pesky human. Whether Silas's parents would thank him for this remained to be seen.

Delphie opened the door and smiled at him, making the breath seize up in his lungs and a strange ringing commence in his ears. "Hi," she said, a shy note to her voice that he found curiously endearing. The scent of fried chicken drifted to him and he inhaled deeply, dragging a little bit of her scent in with it as well. Vanilla and lemons, an intriguing combination.

"That smells delicious," he said, referring to her more than the meal.

"Come on in," she told him, widening the door to allow him entrance.

He held out a bottle of wine he'd picked up earlier when he'd been out. "For you," he said. She'd left her bottle on the back porch last night, so rather than risking a bad choice he'd simply bought the same thing.

"Thank you," she murmured, blushing slightly once more. She started toward the kitchen. "Have you had a good day?"

He trailed along behind her, enjoying the swing of her hips. She wore a pair of black pants, a light blue sweater and a chunky necklace that drew the eye to her breasts. Oh, hell. Who was he kidding? She could be wearing a garbage bag and his eyes would be drawn to her breasts.

Because they were magnificent.

"I have," he confirmed. "I went to the grocery store for a few essentials—"

"Like beer," she interjected.

"Like beer," he confirmed. She uncorked the wine, poured him a glass, then handed it to him. "And I put up the Christmas tree and a few decorations. I taught the cat a new trick. Exciting stuff," he told her. "What about you?"

"I, too, had to make a run to the grocery store," she said, shooting him a smile. She started transferring dishes to the dining room table, her movements smooth and seemingly effortless. "And I worked a bit, of course."

"From home?"

She nodded. "Yep, which suits me just fine. After my first assessment, I can do a lot from right here."

And right here was lovely, he had to admit. Though there was plenty of color in her house, the furniture was mostly white. White boards covered the walls and ceilings, contrasting nicely with dark wide-plank pine floors. A couple of old porch posts were stationed on either side of the dining room, separating it from the living room, and she'd opted for open kitchen cabinets which were filled with lots of old dishes. Rather than a lot of pretty houses that were simply decorated for display, hers was livable and functional, accented with repurposed materials and reclaimed woodwork. After a moment, he said as much.

"This is really nice. Did you do some of it yourself?"

She gestured for him to sit and heap his plate, then

chuckled once. "I did it *all* myself, thank you very much."

He felt his eyes widen. "All?"

"My dad was a carpenter," she explained, ladling gravy over her mashed potatoes. "Retired now, of course, but I spent a lot of time with him when I was younger."

Unbelievably impressed, he set his fork aside and stared at her. "Are you telling me that you know how to use power tools?"

She grinned and lifted a brow. "Do you want to see my nail gun?"

He shook his head and tore off another bite of chicken. "Forget the dairy cow, too," he said in wonder. "You are a gem among women. And you're a helluva cook," he added thickly around a mouthful of chicken. "This is amazing."

"Thank you," she told him, looking pleased. "So what about you? Had you always planned on joining the military?"

Silas laughed. "You're telling me you don't know the answer to that question? My mother hasn't given you everything but my pant size already?"

Her blue eyes twinkled. "Thirty, thirty-six."

He choked on a bite of mashed potatoes. "You're freaking kidding me," he said, stunned. "Tell me you guessed."

"She only mentioned it because you're such a hard fit," she told him.

Silas looked heavenward. Good Lord, what else had his mother told her? How he used to think that the bank tellers in drive-thru windows lived in those little boxes? How he'd once wanted a mustache like his father so much that he'd drawn it on with a Sharpie? How he'd been so nervous before his first day of school he'd puked all over his teacher's shoes?

His gaze slid to her once more and a bark of dry laughter rumbled up his throat. He had a terrible feeling he should have been paying better attention to what his mother had been saying about him to Delphie, because he was pretty damned certain she'd been listening when the Master Manipulator—better known as Helen Davenport—had been talking about *him*.

DELPHIE LAUGHED AT HIS suddenly wary expression. "You don't have to look so worried," she said. "Your mother only ever had wonderful things to say about you."

"That's what I'm afraid of," he remarked grimly. "She's been doing the hard sell, hasn't she?"

Delphie felt her lips twitch and hesitated long enough for him to swear under his breath. "She's been very proud of you, that's all."

He rolled his eyes. "Nothing is more embarrassing than having your mother interfere with your game," he said with a put-upon sigh.

"You're doing well enough on your own," she conceded, quirking a brow at him.

He looked up at her and smiled, the grin eternally slow and lethally sexy and filled with so much heat she felt her toes curl once again. "That's good to know," he remarked.

"So what about me?" she asked. "You haven't been getting the hard sell on me?"

"I have." He winced. "But to tell you the truth, I didn't pay that much attention."

She felt a droll smile curl her lips. "Because anyone your mother would pitch couldn't be someone you'd be interested in?"

He poked his tongue in his cheek. "Are you psychic or am I just that easy to read?"

"Neither," she told him. "I am diametrically opposed to anyone my mother suggests, as well." She took a sip of wine. "But you never answered my question."

"What was that?"

"Had you always wanted to join the military?"

He nodded. "Always," he confirmed. "The year I got a G.I. Joe for Christmas changed the course of my life," he joked, smiling. "Aside from being away from home, I love everything about it. I love knowing that I'm doing something that's honorable, that I believe in. That I'm standing in the gap, fighting for something bigger than myself, until the next group of like-minded men come along." He peered at her above the rim of his glass. "Sounds trite, I know, but..."

"It doesn't sound trite at all," she said, swallowing. It was noble and good and she was thankful there were men like him willing to serve.

"So no wedding festivities tonight?" he asked. "Don't they typically have a rehearsal and dinner or something?"

"Actually, no. A friend of Lena's is performing the service and it's very straightforward. She goes in, we follow. They say the I-dos and then we party."

He lifted one shoulder in a shrug. "Sounds simple enough."

"Instead of doing the stag party and bachelorette thing, Lena and Theo are partying together tonight, hosting their own intimate wake for the passing of their single days."

He nodded. "Interesting idea. They sound like a very...different couple."

Finished eating, she settled more firmly into her seat.

She laughed softly and rubbed the bridge of her nose. "They're perfect for each other. It's disgusting."

"How long have they been dating?"

"Just a few months."

"So long enough for the new to still be there, but not long enough to discover any annoying habits." He nodded once. "Probably for the best."

She eyed him speculatively. "You sound like you've put a good deal of thought into this. Any particular reason you aren't married yet? Don't have enough land for the livestock you anticipate as a dowry?" she quipped.

Silas laughed again, the sound sexy and soothing, one that she knew she could easily get used to hearing. His gaze tangled with hers. "Honestly, I've just never met the right girl and haven't had time to truly look. I'm not opposed to it, if that's what you're asking. I'm not so attached to being single that I don't ever want to get married." He paused, looking thoughtful. "But I'd rather be alone than married to someone who wasn't right, you know?"

She did know. She had a couple of friends who'd rushed into marriage—more thrilled with having a wedding than having a husband—only to realize that the men they'd promised to love till death did them part weren't as wonderful as they had originally imagined.

He blew out a small breath. "And when I make a promise, then…I make a promise." A little frown creased his brow. "I think too many people go into a marriage believing there's a quick way out of it. That the vows are just pretty words, not the oath it's intended to be."

My goodness, Delphie thought, staring at him with a new appreciation. A man of his word. How novel.

He looked up and caught her staring at him, then an adorably self-conscious smile curled his lips. "What?" he said. "You think I'm old-fashioned, don't you?"

"I do," she said with nod. "And I think the world could use a lot more men like you."

Pity she wasn't going to have time to get to know him better, she thought, a pinprick of disappointment nicking her heart. Silas Davenport was handsome and funny, smart and charming and held on to antiquated beliefs that she happened to share. He was good, she realized. Genuinely good. And good guys were getting harder and harder to find.

Thankfully, though, she still had time to get to know him as well as she could.

She looked up then and caught him staring hungrily at her mouth, as though the dinner they'd just shared had been nice but not enough. Heat flashed over the tops of her thighs and a breathless gasp slipped out of her lungs. Her palms suddenly itched to touch him, to see if the skin on the back of his neck was as warm as it looked. If it could possibly taste as good as she'd imagined.

She'd been thinking about him all day. Anticipated seeing him again more and more with each passing second. She'd been keenly aware of her body, the way the air felt moving in and out of her lungs, the tight fit of her bra, the slide of silk over her hips. She'd worked, yes, but she'd also spent a great deal of time peeking out of her window, trying to catch a glimpse of him. And she'd spent just as much time watching the clock, waiting until the hour hand struck five and the countdown to having him had officially started.

Yes, she still had a little time to get to know him.

And if they were naked, then all the better.

5

SILAS KNEW THE EXACT moment he was going to get lucky. Something in her gaze shifted, became more open, less guarded…and a lot hotter.

"Thank you for dinner," he told her. "That's the best meal I've had in a very long time."

"You're welcome," she said. "It was the least I could do considering you're braving the wedding for me. You're going to make me look considerably less pitiable and for that I am forever grateful."

"It's nothing," he said, waving negligently. "I think you and I could find something to laugh at anywhere." He leaned forward. "And just think of all the material we're going to have to work with at a wedding. There's certain to be a crazy uncle, a drunken aunt and a too-blunt grandmother to provide entertainment." His gaze tangled purposely with hers. "And as an added bonus, I get to dance with you. Win, win," he told her.

"How did you know about Uncle Harry?" she quipped, her eyes widening.

"It's a given. There's always a crazy uncle at these things."

"Are you a good dancer?" she asked, her gaze lingering on his mouth again. Honestly, if she didn't stop looking at him like that, he was going to clear the table and have her for dessert.

He studied her for a moment, let his gaze drift over her face, along the slim line of her throat, the gentle swells of her breasts. And honestly, why didn't he do just that? They both knew that he wasn't here to eat fried chicken—he was here to make a meal out of her.

He stood and offered her his hand. "Why don't you turn the music up and find out?"

She visibly swallowed, then bit her bottom lip to keep from smiling. She knew where this was going. What sort of dance he really had in mind.

And she wanted it, too, otherwise he wouldn't be here.

With a simple inclination of her head, she picked up the remote control to the stereo and increased the volume. The music was bluesy and low, the perfect background for making love. The next second, she placed her hand in his and he drew her close, savoring the feel of her body next to his. Soft, warm, womanly. He inhaled, tasting her scent—musky with a citrusy finish. Something inside of him tightened and released, as though a lock had been thrown, the tumbler rolling into place.

She felt...*right.* Better. More significant than any other woman he'd ever held before.

"You smell nice," he said, whispering the compliment into her ear. Gratifyingly, she shivered and murmured a thanks. "Who is this?" he asked her, nodding toward the stereo. He wrapped his arm more snugly around her waist, knowing that it was going to make him harder and she was going to be able to tell. He could feel the tension gathering along her spine, her need pinging his, making it all the more potent, all the more intense.

"Marc Broussard."

"I like him."

She drew back and looked up at him. "I'm breaking my own rules for you, you know," she said, as if unable to prevent the disclaimer.

"Rules?" he scoffed playfully. "What rules?"

"I typically have to know someone better before I—" She struggled to find the right word.

"Make fried chicken for them?" he helpfully supplied the euphemism.

She chuckled, lowered her gaze. "Yes. I ordinarily have to know someone a little bit longer before I…make f-fried chicken for them." He loved her smile, the way her ripe lips curled just so. Her lashes were long and lush and painted shadows beneath her eyes. He loved that, too.

He grinned down at her. "So what you're trying to tell me is that I'm special."

"Something like that, yes," she confirmed.

"You're pretty damned extraordinary yourself," he told her. And she was. She was smart and creative, funny and warm-hearted. Aside from being unbelievably attracted to her, he genuinely liked her, Silas realized. She'd been an instant friend, which was rarer than this phenomenal appeal. He might have thought about that little realization and its significance if she hadn't chosen that exact moment to nuzzle her nose along his throat.

Sensation bolted through him, snapping the thin line of restraint he'd been holding on to. He drew back and kissed her, let his lips slide purposefully over hers, feeling the petal softness of her mouth against his. She bloomed, opening for him, and he slipped his tongue into her mouth, delving into the soft recesses, tasting her, sampling her, dragging her into the pit of lust he'd found himself in since meeting her.

She responded in kind, wrapped her arms more tightly around him, sliding her thumb along his jaw, behind her ear, into his hair. Her mouth was hot and languid, insistent and lazy, and he couldn't get enough of her, couldn't hold back. The intensity of the need—the unnamed emotion attached to the need specifically— should have terrified him, yet it didn't.

She breathed a sigh into his mouth that was part surrender, part relief, and with a little jump, wrapped her arms more firmly around his neck and her legs around his waist.

A minute later, she'd directed him to the bedroom and thirty seconds beyond that, he had her naked. Curly black hair spilled over a stark white pillow. Pale pink nipples pouted for his kiss. A smooth belly, the flare of womanly hips and a thatch of dark curls between her creamy thighs called to him.

Beautiful.

Achingly so.

Though he'd been sexually active since his teens and had never doubted his ability to please a woman, he was unaccountably nervous, felt like an anxious virgin hiding behind a large erection and more bravado than skill all over again. She was small and perfectly made, and he wanted to do this right, to make her thankful that she was breaking her rules for him. More than anything he knew he was going to want more of her *fried chicken* and, irrationally, he believed additional helpings were dependent upon this performance.

He bent and took a dusky nipple into his mouth,

shaping her breast in his hand as he did so. She sighed a gratifying mewl of pleasure and tunneled her fingers into his hair. She arched up, giving him more, a silent offering, one he was more than willing to take. He licked a path to her other breast, circling the nipple with his tongue before pulling it deeply into his mouth. She made that noise again—the one that made him want to beat his chest and roar—and then slid her hands down over his back, tracing his spine.

The feel of her small, capable fingers against his skin sent gooseflesh skittering along the backs of his legs, and when her hand glided ever so innocently over his hip, then found its way between his legs, he almost came undone.

Or just came.

She worked him against her palm, skimming the tip of his engorged penis with her thumb, then clasped him once more and worked the skin along his dick from root to tip. Every stroke of her soft hand against him sent sensation hurtling through him, made his balls tighten and toes dig into the mattress. Taking a page out of her book, Silas slid his own hand down her abdomen, found the dewy curls between her thighs and deftly parted her nether lips. She was hot and wet against his fingers and the first brush of his thumb over her clit made her buck against his hand.

He smiled, rather pleased with himself.

She palmed his balls, pulling another hiss from between his teeth, and his smile capsized. She leaned forward and kissed his shoulder, dipped her tongue into the hollow of his collarbone—who knew that was an erogenous zone?—and then slid her wonderful lips along his throat. She nipped at his ear and worked herself against him as he slipped a finger deep inside her.

She gasped again, every sound of pleasure an affirmation that this was right. She stroked him harder as he massaged her clit, then she shifted and lifted her hips.

"Please," she said. "I need—"

Truer words had never been spoken, Silas thought. He needed, too. He snagged his wallet from his pants at the foot of the bed and took out a condom, opened the packet and then swiftly rolled the protection into place. His gaze tangled with hers as he nudged against her, poised at the entrance of her womanhood. He didn't know what stopped him, why he paused. He only knew that it was imperative that she see him, that they commemorate the moment with a shared look. Her eyes were feverish and glazed, her mouth swollen and rosy from his kisses, her nipples erect and waiting. She was beautiful and perfect and right, and when he pushed into her, seated himself firmly between her milky thighs, he knew he'd never felt more at home anywhere.

And instinctively he knew he never would again.

DELPHIE'S BREATH ESCAPED in a long, desperate hiss as Silas came into her. He was big and hard and felt so unbelievably perfect. She'd heard of hot, mindless sex before, but had never truly had it until right this instant. From the moment he'd kissed her she'd completely lost control. She'd fed at his mouth, clawed away his clothes and squirmed shamelessly against him, utterly desperate to feel him inside of her. To put her hands on his bare flesh.

He loomed over her like a dark angel—black hair, black eyes and a smile that was as wicked as Satan himself. He looked at her as though he didn't know what to make of her, as though she were a mystery he had to solve, as though he desperately wanted a peek inside her head as well as a trip inside her body.

And she loved it. Relished it. Savored it.

She rocked her hips beneath him, taking him farther into her body and watched as he set his jaw. It made her feel powerful and less reckless because this was without a doubt the most out of control she'd ever been.

She didn't do this. She didn't *do* complete strangers.

But he didn't feel like a stranger. He felt perfect.

He bent his dark head and pulled her breast into his mouth once again, laving her budded nipple with his tongue.

Her feminine muscles clamped harder around him and a purely masculine sound escaped between his lips. It was music to her ears. She licked a determined path along his neck and breathed into his ear, then nipped at his earlobe and grinned when she felt him swell inside her.

He moved faster, pumping in and out of her, while feeding at her breasts. He was everywhere at once—on top of her, inside her. She found his mouth again, kissing him as he upped the tempo between their joined bodies.

She felt the first flash of impending release build in her sex and held him tighter. She grabbed the twin globes of his ass and drew her legs back, giving him better access.

He pushed harder, faster, then faster still and she could feel her breath getting stuck in her throat and she gasped and bucked wildly beneath him.

She needed— She wanted—

He reached down between them, found the little kernel of pleasure nestled at the top of her sex and pressed.

She came.

She dragged in a huge breath, but couldn't let it go. Lights danced behind her closed lids, every muscle in her body contracted and she fisted around him, coming harder than she ever had before in her life.

The orgasm was brighter, better and more satisfying than anything she'd ever experienced. She felt herself tighten around him again, then he set his jaw and pushed her harder, her tingling breasts absorbing his manic thrusts.

Three seconds later, he growled low in his throat and shuddered violently. His eyes closed, seemingly from the weight of pleasure, and a slow smile shaped his lips.

After a moment, he looked down at her, a wonderingly confused but satisfied look on his face. "Well," he said. "I'm glad we got that out of the way."

"Out of the way?" she repeated, feigning offense though she knew exactly what he was talking about.

He carefully withdrew, disposed of the condom with a tissue from beside the bed, then curled up next to her.

"Yeah," he said. "Because next time I intend to do a proper job of it."

She laughed and pressed a kiss against his naked shoulder. "You mean to tell me you didn't give me your best?" she teased.

She felt him chuckle beside her. "I can always do better."

If he did any better she didn't know if she'd survive it. "I like a man who wants to improve."

He slid a finger beneath the swell of her breast, making her shiver. "And I like a woman who's so into me she doesn't remember getting naked."

"How do you know I don't remember?"

"That telling frown I saw just a minute ago. It's the

same look my dad gets when he walks into a room and then forgets what he went in there for."

What was the point in denying it? She didn't remember getting naked. She only remembered how nice it was after she'd gotten there. How much she'd loved the feel of him deep inside her, the delicious draw and drag between their joined bodies, the slip of his tongue along the base of her throat.

It was *wonderful*. Intoxicating. Potentially habit forming.

"You know what I think we should do?" she asked.

"What?"

"Take the rest of that wine and go get in the hot tub."

He chuckled. "Admit it. You just want see me naked."

She merely shrugged. "Turn about's fair play, right? You certainly got an eyeful last night."

"I didn't see anything," he said. "Though I wanted to," he qualified. "Damned bubbles."

"I was mortified."

He laughed softly. "I know. It was most entertaining."

"Thank you ladies and gentlemen," she said, deadpan. "I'm here every night. *Bada bing*."

He nuzzled her neck. "You have the most interesting sense of humor."

She frowned, not altogether certain that was a compliment. "Is that a charitable way of saying that I'm weird?"

"No, it's a nice way of saying that you're fascinating."

She blinked, absorbing that statement, and felt a ripple of happiness eddy through her. She rather liked being fascinating. "Oh."

"You still want to go get in the hot tub?" he asked, pressing another kiss to the underside of her jaw. His hand found her breast and played lazily with her nipple. She felt him twitch against her thigh, rising to the challenge, as it were, once again. Her belly quickened in response, warmth engulfing her core.

"Nah," Delphie told him. "I've got wine here and you're already naked. Win, win."

"Come here," he said, laughing softly, rolling her toward him. "I'll let you have your wicked way with me."

As offers went, it was a pretty damned good one.

6

"THANKS SO MUCH FOR doing this," Delphie said the next day as they entered the church. She wore a red velvet dress with white fur trim and a matching Santa hat adorned with a sprig of holly. Her sister evidently had a unique sense of style and it was all Silas could do to keep from laughing at Delphie's pained expression when he'd gone over to pick her up this afternoon.

"No problem," he told her, smiling down at her. He just looked forward to taking it off her. He'd ended up spending the night with her last night and he'd awoken to the feel of a soft rump against his groin and a softer breast in his hand.

This could potentially be the best Christmas of his life.

She'd had a few wedding-related things to do this morning and he'd needed to get his Christmas shopping done, so they'd parted ways after a quick breakfast. It had been so easy being with her; he was trying to pinpoint the exact reason why that was.

Ultimately, he'd decided, it was simply her. She had no expectations, was funny and charming and the most responsive, enthusiastic bed partner he'd ever had. In fact, he could quite easily see himself becoming addicted to her.

Simply put, she was easy company and he enjoyed every minute he spent with her, in and out of bed.

That had never happened before. He typically either liked a girl well enough but found her lacking in the bedroom, or vice versa. This was the first time he'd ever found the total package.

How ironic that it was the girl his mother had been telling him about.

He watched the wedding party come down the aisle to the tune of "Jingle Bells," then everyone stood and the bride made her entrance on her father's arm to "Santa, Baby." He grinned and happened to glance at Delphie, who was looking as long-suffering as it was possible to be without appearing jealous of her sister, and she gave a helpless shrug.

Ten minutes later—after the bride and groom had promised to never let the sun set on an argument—the wedding was over and the reception had begun.

He quickly found Delphie and handed her a drink. "Too bad there's no hot tub to drink it in, eh?" he teased.

She downed the rum and eggnog in one gulp. "Hit me again," she said, shuddering. "Here comes my grandmother. I'm going to need it."

The old woman moved fast for her age, and her faded blue eyes fastened on Silas with a keen sort of awareness that made him acutely uncomfortable. It was as if the old woman had witnessed every depraved thing he'd done to her granddaughter last night and this morning and was going to share it with the room at large. "You must be Delphie's new young man."

"Silas Davenport," he introduced himself while Delphie shrunk with embarrassment. He wrapped his arm around her, drawing her closer to his side. "And I hope that she's as much mine as I am hers," he said.

Beside him, Delphie choked, but the ploy worked. The grandmother went from getting ready to give Delphie the you'll-get-your-turn-at-the-alter spiel to obvious happiness.

The older woman preened. "We're awfully proud of our Delphie."

"Of course," he said. "She's a remarkable woman. And she makes the best fried chicken I've ever eaten."

Delphie glared up him and flattened her lips to keep from laughing.

"Oh, she's a wonderful cook," her grandmother said. "She learned that from me, you know," the older woman went on, completely oblivious to the true meaning of the conversation. "I like to soak my chicken in buttermilk. Makes it more tender, you see. And the longer the better."

"That's right, Granny," she said, nearly choking. She darted a glance beyond the older woman's shoulder, pretending to see someone she needed to talk to. "Oh, look, there's Uncle Harry." She jerked Silas in her crazy uncle's direction. "I've been meaning to tell him something. See you later, Granny."

Looking a bit baffled, her grandmother merely smiled and nodded goodbye. As soon as they were away from her, Delphie whirled on him and giggled. "The best fried chicken you've ever had, huh?"

"Without question," he told her, smiling. He led her onto the dance floor, curling her into his arms as Bing Crosby's "White Christmas" suddenly drifted through the speakers. She smelled wonderful, he thought. Like a lemon pound cake—which was probably not all that complimentary, but delicious all the same.

"I'm quite flattered. You're not half bad yourself."

"Half bad?" he remarked, his eyes rounding as he sent her into a twirl. "Clearly I'm not trying hard enough."

"Yes, but you're steadily improving," she told him, "and that's what's important."

He wanted to take her right now, Silas thought. He wanted to flip that ridiculous dress up over her hips and slip into her from behind. He wanted to feel her breasts pebble against his hands and suck on her neck while he pounded into her, her sweet ass cradling his groin. He cast her a brooding glance. He'd even let her leave the hat on.

She saw him watching her and a wary smile shaped her mouth. "Do I even want to know what you're thinking?"

He purposely licked his lips, allowed his fingers to slip along the side of her breast. She gasped, her gaze finding his. "I'm thinking about fried chicken and the likelihood of having some right now."

She swallowed hard and he watched as her pulse fluttered wildly at the base of her throat. "Right now?"

He was suddenly so hard he could scarcely think of anything else. Red was her color. She'd put it on her lips as well, and the image of her mouth encircling him, sliding along his dick, was so vivid he actually stumbled over his own feet. "Right damned *now.*"

With a nonchalant shrug he'd remember forever, she threaded her fingers through his and tugged him toward the door.

DELPHIE WAS SO SHOCKED at herself she didn't know what to do. One minute she'd been enjoying Silas's quick but unsolicited rescue from her grandmother—he couldn't have said anything better had she scripted the line for him herself—and their ensuing dance. The next, he'd mentioned fried chicken, and her sex had started throbbing right along with her frantically beating heart.

Who gives a damn about the wedding? Delphie thought, and her breasts grew heavier and heavier with need. She just wanted to have the honeymoon over and over again.

With Silas.

She led him downstairs to a little-used bathroom and she'd no more than closed the door before she felt him behind her, lifting her dress, his hot fingers against the backs of her thighs.

A thrill whipped through her.

She bent over and parted her legs, then cast him a glance over her shoulder.

"I want you so bad I can barely think straight," he said, making the confession as he slid a finger against her slick folds.

She gasped and wiggled against him. "It's the fur on the dress, isn't it? It's sort of got a porn-star quality."

He laughed into her ear, then suckled her neck. She heard the telltale sound of a condom package tearing, the whine of his zipper and a second later she felt him pushing against her nether lips.

Her mouth opened in a soundless gasp and she felt her muscles clench, readying for him. She arched her back and bent forward, giving him better access. With a guttural groan of masculine satisfaction, he slid into her.

The breath hitched out of her lungs and she tightened around him and pressed her hands against the door. He slid out and pushed again and she could tell that he was holding back, that he was afraid of hurting her.

But that wasn't what hurt.

"Don't be gentle," she said, clenching her teeth against the need hammering against her. "Take me how you really want me."

He gave a startled little laugh and then bent forward and breathed into her ear. "I do like the fur," he said. "It's hot. And you look good in red. Like Santa's sexy little helper."

He grabbed hold of her hips and pounded into her. It was wild and manic, hot and dirty, and to her immense surprise, she found she really wanted it that way.

He did this to her, Delphie thought. He made her want him like this. He pistoned in and out of her, harder and faster, then faster still. She absorbed his thrusts and worked herself against him, arched her head back when it got to be too much and he bent forward and bit her shoulder, a light nip, but she liked it so much it made her vision blacken around the edges. He reached around and massaged her clit, upped the tempo and nipped at her neck.

"You're…improving," she gasped, feeling the first bit of climax dawning in her quivering, anxious sex.

"You know…what they…say about…practice," he said, taking her harder and harder. He was big and hard and wonderful and the only thing she regretted about this was not being able to put her hands on him. She loved the way he felt beneath her palms—the salty taste of his smooth skin, the texture of his male nipple against her tongue. She felt his tautened balls slapping against her aching skin, his huge hand on her hip and a masterful finger stroking her clit.

It was too much, too perfect, too…everything.

The orgasm swept her up, then pushed her down and her muscles clamped so hard she felt him jerk and groan behind her.

"Delphie," he breathed, her name a curse. "You're killing me."

She sagged against the door, her legs weak, and savored the lingering pulses of release. "Good," she breathed. "Because I don't want to die alone."

She meant it in the figurative sense, but realized the double meaning as soon as the words left her mouth. He came an instant later and held her tighter, then kissed the nape of her neck. "You won't," he said. "At this point I'm even willing to give up the goats."

Delphie laughed, missing him already.

7

THOUGH SHE'D INVITED him over for Christmas dinner with her family, Silas had ultimately refused. He tried to tell himself that he didn't want to intrude, but the truth was he was beginning to suspect he needed a little distance from Delphie to try to get his head back in the game.

Because at this point, he'd already lost it.

He'd known her three days, would be boarding a plane first thing in the morning and though he always dreaded leaving, it was never quite like this.

Right now the idea of being so far from Delphie made him feel utterly miserable, which was cause for concern on more levels than he cared to count.

He couldn't be this invested in someone he'd only known three days, could he? Surely not. Granted, it felt as if he'd known her a lot longer than that and she was by far the most interesting person he'd ever met. And the sex...

His balls tightened just thinking about it.

He couldn't get enough of her.

He looked at her mouth and instantly craved her. She made him crazy with wanting, and the perpetual need to slip out of his skin and into hers only worsened the more time they spent together. And, of course, he wanted to spend every second with her, so that wasn't helping matters, either.

He could tell that she'd hated leaving him this morning, but he'd assured her he'd be fine. He'd wrapped presents for his parents and sister and left them under the tree, and he'd picked up a little something for Delphie yesterday when he'd been out, as well. It was a small pendant made of blue sea glass that perfectly matched the shade of her eyes.

He'd just taken the bread out of the oven when he heard her knock at the door. "You cooked," she said, her eyes sparkling with delight. "You didn't have to do that."

"I wanted to," he said simply. "Although you're probably not very hungry."

Her gaze slid over him slowly as she set aside a bag and shrugged out of her coat. "Actually, I've been thinking about eating all day."

Her eyes lingered on his groin, alerting him to what exactly she'd been thinking of eating, and every bit of the moisture evaporated from his mouth.

"I've got a special Christmas treat for you," she said.

"You do?" Did that hoarse voice belong to him?

She gave him a gentle shove, sending him toppling onto the couch. "Yep."

She retrieved the bag she'd brought in and handed it to him. The scent of oranges and yeast and icing instantly enveloped him and he grinned. "You made the orange rolls?"

"I tried," she said. "I'm not sure they're exactly what you're used to, but…" She pulled a little shrug, then dropped to her knees in front of him. His zipper whined as he withdrew the sticky treat and she waited for him to take his first bite before she wrapped her hot mouth around his dick and sucked.

He came embarrassingly close to coming instantly and his eyes rolled back in his head.

She worked the slippery skin against her hand, licked and sucked and lapped and laved. She massaged his balls, paid particular attention to the tender area beneath the full head of his penis. From the unbelievably happy look on her face, she was enjoying eating him as much as he was loving the orange roll.

He'd never look at the dessert the same way.

As he popped the last bite into his mouth, she sucked harder. Then he came. Her eyes met his as she lapped him up, savoring the taste of his release.

"Silas?"

"Hmm?"

"Merry Christmas."

He dropped his head against the back of the couch and chuckled softly.

Oh, yes, it had been after all.

"I've got something for you," he said later that evening, after he'd reciprocated her earlier gesture. Delphie was spent and boneless and dreading the morning.

"You do? You didn't have to do that."

"I know," he said. "That's what makes it a present."

She laughed against his chest. "I thought you'd just given me your present."

"I think you'll like this one better," he said.

She smiled. "Oh, I doubt that very seriously."

He tsked. "You haven't even seen it yet." He reached under the Christmas tree and pulled a small package out for her, then handed it to her.

Damn. Her gaze flew to his. He'd gotten her a *real* present. She'd just made him some orange rolls and given him a blow job. She hadn't expected this. "Oh," she said. "Thank you."

"Aren't you going to open it?"

Fingers trembling, she did just that. "Oh, Silas," she breathed. "Sea glass."

"I thought of you when I saw it."

"Thank you," she said, more touched than she could imagine. "It's beautiful."

"It's the color of your eyes."

"You don't have to flatter me, you know. I'm a sure thing."

He stared at her. "You need to learn to take a compliment."

Maybe so, but this felt as though it changed things. Their brief but glorious relationship had been fun and uncomplicated and she thought she'd done a good job of keeping her feelings in check. But this little token changed things, made her realize just how much she truly…cared for him.

In the morning he was going to leave again, which in theory had made him safe. But she didn't feel safe now, and he damned sure wouldn't be safe when he went back to Iraq.

She was going to worry and be miserable and there wasn't anything she could do about it. Too late she realized that this had never been uncomplicated, that she could never disengage her heart like that.

Silas Davenport, damn him, was special. He always had been, whether she'd been willing to admit it or not.

"Here," he said. "Let me put it on you."

She turned and felt his fingers brush the back of her

neck. Another shiver eddied through her and she felt her eyes burn.

Oh, hell.

"Your parents are really going to hate that they've missed you," she said, looking for a subject change.

"I hate that I've missed them, too," he told her. "But I have certainly enjoyed spending time with you." He studied her, smiled. "You're fun."

She ducked her head and tucked a strand of hair behind her ear. "Thank you."

"See," he said. "This is what I love about you. You give me the best Christmas present of my life without batting a lash. I give you a compliment and you blush six shades of red."

"You know what I love about you?" she asked.

"I hope that it's something truly depraved," he murmured, his gaze drifting over her.

"I love how you feel…inside me."

"I can hook you up," he said, rolling on top of her.

Delphie leaned forward and licked a path up his throat. "Make it count, soldier. We're on a time line here."

He did.

8

"YOU SERIOUSLY DIDN'T have to do this," Silas said as they stood in the airport. He had his duffel packed, his papers ready. Everything was a go.

Only he didn't want to.

"Nonsense," she said briskly, a wobbly smile on her face. "You're a friend, Silas, and friends don't let friends drive themselves to the airport."

A friend. He knew that was true, but for the first time in his life he wanted to be so much more. He wasn't exactly sure when it had happened, but Delphie Moreau had burrowed under his skin and attached herself to his heart. Was he in love with her? Honestly, he didn't know. He'd never been in love before and had nothing to compare it to, no frame of reference.

But he knew he cared about her, that he didn't want to leave her and that the idea of anyone else eating his fried chicken set his teeth on edge and made him want to break things.

If it wasn't love, then it was damned close.

She'd made arrangements to return the rental to a place in Folly Beach and had driven him to the airport herself. It meant that he got to spend more time with her, of course, but he suspected it was going to make saying goodbye all the more difficult.

Shit.

How had this happened? At what point had she become so damned important? His heart was beating so fast in his chest he was afraid it was going to burst right through. His palms and feet tingled and he had a horrible premonition that when he tried to walk away he wasn't going to be able to do it, that she would have to make the move first.

"Any idea when you'll get to come home again?" she asked. She posed the question lightly, as though it didn't matter, but her mouth was white around the edges and she shifted from one foot to the other, as though she was about to come out of her skin.

"My tour is up in two months," he said. "I'll definitely come home for a little while then."

She smiled. "Is it going to send you into a panic if I say I'd like to see you?"

Relief poured through him, loosening his tight limbs. "Not at all." He paused, darted a look at her. "I was actually hoping that I could call you, that you'd write."

She nodded, her eyes twinkling with tentative happiness. "I'd like that very much," she said.

Damn, this was hard. He had an entirely new appreciation for the guys who left behind wives and significant others now. This was horrible. Like lopping off an appendage.

She raised up onto her tippy toes and kissed him. Without hesitation, he wrapped his arms around her, lifted her off the floor and deepened the kiss. He poured every bit of his feelings into the mating of their mouths, showed her everything he didn't have the words to say.

Catcalls and applause suddenly rang out and he reluctantly pulled away and rested his forehead against hers.

"Be careful over there," she said, her voice thick. Her eyes were bright with unshed tears she tried to keep him from seeing.

He nodded and made himself turn and walk away, and every step that took him farther from her became harder and harder to make.

Bloody damned hell.

WELL, THIS ABSOLUTELY SUCKED, Delphie thought as she watched Silas disappear into the security line. She told herself to move, but couldn't seem to get her feet to cooperate.

She'd realized late last night that this was going to be more terrible than she'd suspected. He'd mentioned his early departure and her heart had given a painful little squeeze. She'd ignored it then because she hadn't wanted to do anything that was a) going to clue him in to her sudden discomfort or b) ruin what was left of their time together by alluding to feelings it should be impossible to have.

She'd only known him three days. People didn't fall in three days. Did they? Rational, sane people? Ordinary levelheaded people? Not to say that she was any of those things—clearly she wasn't, otherwise she wouldn't have this huge lump in her throat—but it certainly lessened her ability to make fun of her sister's drive-thru love connection if it was the case.

The idea of not seeing him, not tasting him, not hearing that wicked laugh she'd grown so attached to made something in her chest twist and squeeze. She loved the sound of his heartbeat beneath her ear, the feel of his big hands sliding over her bare back. She liked kissing the soft spot beneath his jaw, loved the smell of his skin.

Two months before she'd see him again? Geez, it already felt like an eternity and he'd been gone less than a minute.

This sure as hell didn't bode well for the next sixty days.

With a deep bolstering breath, Delphie turned and started toward the exit.

"Delphie!"

Silas? Her heart leaped into her throat. She turned, only to see him running toward her. She frowned up at him as he skidded to a stop. "What are you doing?" she asked. "Aren't you going to miss your flight?"

"Not if I hurry," he said. His gaze searched hers and he seemed at a loss for the right words, which was bizarre in and of itself. He pushed his hand through his hair, looked away, then back at her.

"Silas?" she asked, confused. "Is something wrong? Have you forgotten something?"

His dark gaze latched on to hers. "Look, I know this is going to sound crazy, but I need to ask you something."

She nodded. "Okay."

"How do you feel about me?" he wanted to know. "You like me well enough?"

A strangled laugh broke loose in her throat at the absurdity of his question. "I think you know I like you well enough, Silas."

"And if I wasn't leaving right now, would you want to see me again on a regular basis?"

She nodded. Definitely. "I would."

"And if we were seeing each other on a regular basis, then we'd both want exclusivity, right?"

Exclusivity? Was he asking what she thought he was asking? "We would," she said haltingly. She felt a frown wrinkle her brow. "What are you trying to say, Silas?"

"I'm saying I don't want anyone else eating your fried chicken," he said significantly, the words so fierce they sounded as if they'd been pulled out by the roots.

She laughed and inclined her head knowingly. "And does that mean—"

His lips curled with wry humor. "Trust me, I won't be seeing anyone. I promise."

Delphie felt a smile slide over her lips as what he said fully registered. She laughed, her heart full with hope and the possibility of true love. "We just went from fun to serious, didn't we?"

He kissed her again, drew back and sighed. "All that means is that we're going to be having some serious fun when I return."

She smiled up at him. "Good," she said. "I only have one question."

"What's that?"

She hesitated, peeked at him from beneath lowered lashes. "Do you have a hunting dog?"

He guffawed. "No, but I'll get one. And the goats and the dairy cow, if necessary."

"Then we'll be farmers."

"So long as we're together," he said, shrugging as if that was the only thing that mattered.

And it was.

* * * * *

PASSION

For a spicier, decidedly hotter read—
this is your destination for romance!

COMING NEXT MONTH
AVAILABLE DECEMBER 27, 2011

#657 THE PHOENIX
Men Out of Uniform
Rhonda Nelson

#658 BORN READY
Uniformly Hot!
Lori Wilde

#659 STRAIGHT TO THE HEART
Forbidden Fantasies
Samantha Hunter

#660 SEX, LIES AND MIDNIGHT
Undercover Operatives
Tawny Weber

#661 BORROWING A BACHELOR
All the Groom's Men
Karen Kendall

#662 THE PLAYER'S CLUB: SCOTT
The Player's Club
Cathy Yardley

You can find more information on upcoming Harlequin® titles,
free excerpts and more at www.HarlequinInsideRomance.com.

HBCNM1211

REQUEST YOUR FREE BOOKS!
2 FREE NOVELS PLUS 2 FREE GIFTS!

red-hot reads!

Harlequin *Desire*

ALWAYS POWERFUL, PASSIONATE AND PROVOCATIVE.

USA TODAY BESTSELLING AUTHOR

KATHIE DeNOSKY

BRINGS YOU ANOTHER STORY FROM

TEXAS CATTLEMAN'S CLUB: THE SHOWDOWN

Childhood rivals Brad Price and Abigail Langley have found themselves once again in competition, this time for President of the Texas Cattleman's Club. But when Brad's plans are interrupted when his baby niece is suddenly placed under his care, he finds himself asking Abigail for help. As Election Day draws near, will Brad still be going after the Presidency or Abigail's heart? Find out in:

IN BED WITH THE OPPOSITION

Available December wherever books are sold.

Brittany Grayson survived a horrible ordeal at the hands of a serial killer known as The Professional... who's after her now?

Harlequin® Romantic Suspense presents a new installment in Carla Cassidy's reader-favorite miniseries,
LAWMEN OF BLACK ROCK.

Enjoy a sneak peek of
TOOL BELT DEFENDER.

Available January 2012
from Harlequin® Romantic Suspense.

"**B**rittany?" His voice was deep and pleasant and made her realize she'd been staring at him openmouthed through the screen door.

"Yes, I'm Brittany and you must be…" Her mind suddenly went blank.

"Alex. Alex Crawford, Chad's friend. You called him about a deck?"

As she unlocked the screen, she realized she wasn't quite ready yet to allow a stranger inside, especially a male stranger.

"Yes, I did. It's nice to meet you, Alex. Let's walk around back and I'll show you what I have in mind," she said. She frowned as she realized there was no car in her driveway. "Did you walk here?" she asked.

His eyes were a warm blue that stood out against his tanned face and was complemented by his slightly shaggy dark hair. "I live three doors up." He pointed up the street to the Walker home that had been on the market for a while.

"How long have you lived there?"

"I moved in about six weeks ago," he replied as they

walked around the side of the house.

That explained why she didn't know the Walkers had moved out and Mr. Hard Body had moved in. Six weeks ago she'd still been living at her brother Benjamin's house trying to heal from the trauma she'd lived through.

As they reached the backyard she motioned toward the broken brick patio just outside the back door. "What I'd like is a wooden deck big enough to hold a barbecue pit and an umbrella table and, of course, lots of people."

He nodded and pulled a tape measure from his tool belt. "An outdoor entertainment area," he said.

"Exactly," she replied and watched as he began to walk the site. The last thing Brittany had wanted to think about over the past eight months of her life was men. But looking at Alex Crawford definitely gave her a slight flutter of pure feminine pleasure.

Will Brittany be able to heal in the arms of Alex, her hotter-than-sin handyman...or will a second psychopath silence her forever? Find out in
TOOL BELT DEFENDER
Available January 2012
from Harlequin® Romantic Suspense
wherever books are sold.